Also by Mia Dalia

Estate Sale
Smile So Red and Other Tales of Madness
Tell Me a Story
Discordant
Arrokoth
Haven

"*The Muffin Man* is a deliciously sweet 'n' savory neo-noir romp through a playful landscape tied to an intriguing crime story. Nothing here is half-baked. This cunningly-devised and humorous tale will leave you replete."

— Andrew Hook, award-winning editor and author
of *Commercial Book*

"Hilarious and sinister by turns, *The Muffin Man* takes a sweet nursery rhyme, adds a generous dash of murder and mystery, and serves a thriller as cool as cheesecake. A dream crumb true for fans of small-town noir and *The Great British Bake Off*."

— Lindz McLeod, author of *Turducken* and *Sunbathers*

DO YOU KNOW THE MUFFIN MAN?

MIA DALIA

Denver, Colorado

Published in the United States by:
Spaceboy Books LLC
1627 Vine Street
Denver, CO 80206
www.readspaceboy.com

Cover by Mia Dalia

ISBN: 978-1-951393-43-4
First printed February 2025

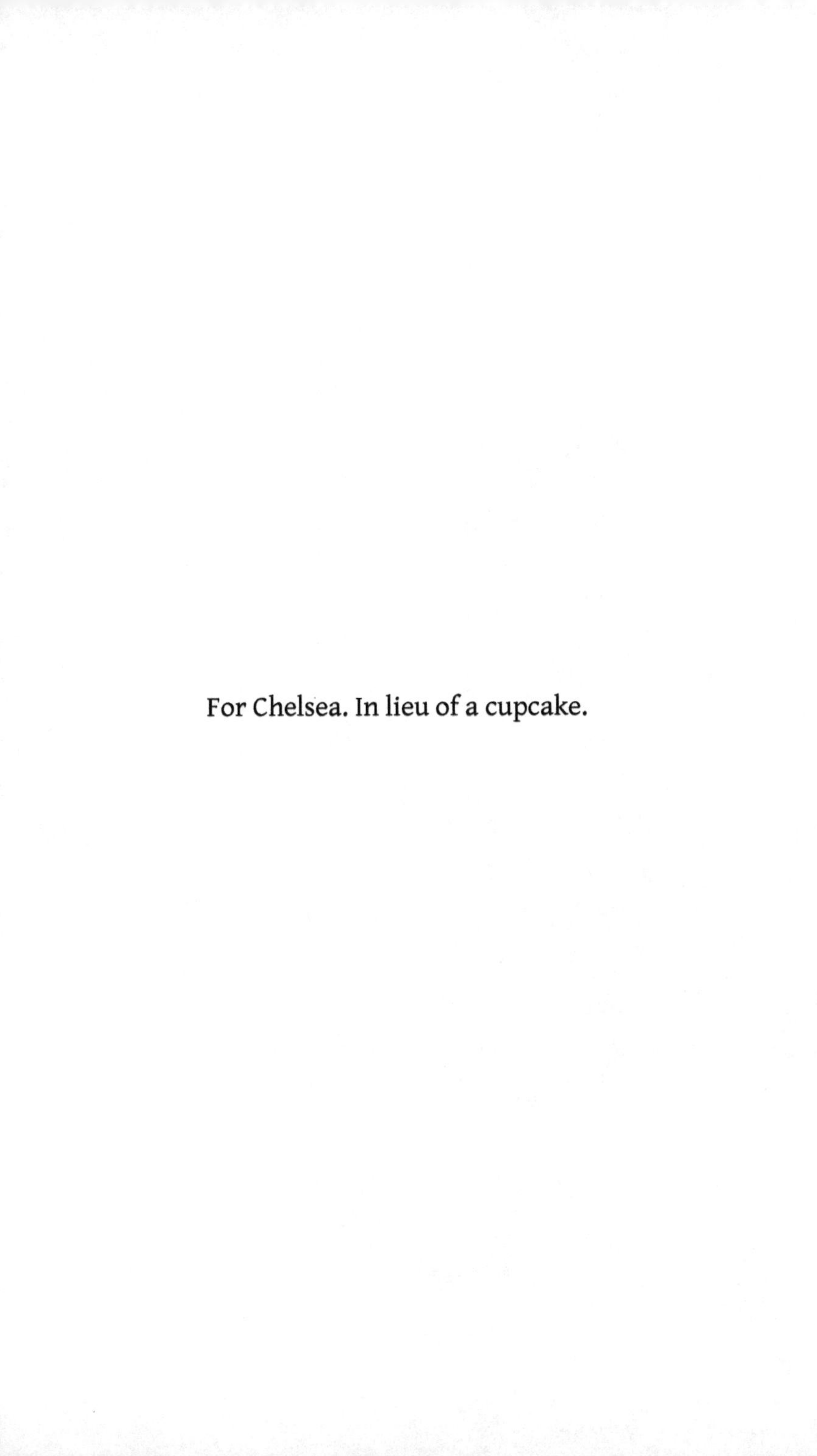

For Chelsea. In lieu of a cupcake.

FOREWORD

What is this thing with me and noir? I don't really read or watch the genre, so I can't quite explain why I enjoy writing it so much. It just *sounds* right to me, and I seem to have a knack for it. My noir stories keep getting published and read. Yay! One of them, "*The Last Best Thing*," was shortlisted for Crime Writers Association's Dagger award in 2024. Double yay!

I guess I just vibe with the shadowy darkness and moodiness of it all. And the trench coat and fedora ascetic do cut a striking silhouette. When it comes to noir, I hear its syncopated rhythms in my mind, like music. And so, I write it. And then I twist it!

And because I'm always interested in breaking out of the "formula" and trying something different, both within and without genres' constraints, and because I normally write very dark stories and my wife occasionally nudges me to do something lighter, and because I seldom let my funny/wacky side out in my writing, and, in no small part, because my wife makes me watch an inordinate amount of baking shows (okay, she doesn't **make me** make me, but it's on TV a lot, so ...), and because I am actually a huge fan of baked goods and muffins in particular (eating them, not watching them being made on TV, that is) ... I wrote this story. Basically, it's mostly my wife's fault, now that I think about it. But she does bake me wonderful things, so I can hardly blame her.

Whether you're a fan of twisted noir, oddball mysteries, and a good pastry, or just curious how all of that can fit together into a book, I'm very glad you have found your way here.

Now then, the question before you is, *Do You Know The Muffin Man?* Read on and let me surprise you.

ONE

The Muffin Man did not appreciate the nursery rhyme. He did not care for its glib jocularity, nor did he like the way it so casually breached his privacy by giving out his address for all the world to see.

Drury Lane had always been so peaceful. Named after its famous English namesake, it didn't have the same storied history, making up for it with quaintness and charm instead. A quiet street culminating in a picturesque cul-de-sac with stately oaks and sprawling elm trees. The Muffin Man and his family had made it their home for a long time. Now that the kids had grown up and fled the nest, and Mrs. Muffin found a more suitable companion in French Baguette, he was on his own, and the house suddenly seemed quite spacious for the first time.

He didn't blame her, not really. They had wonderful decades together, and if in the second act of their life she craved more excitement than he did... well, that was just life, wasn't it? People changed. Or did not change enough. Everyone baked differently. The Muffin Man liked his routines and found solitude to be surprisingly comfortable, like a perfectly broken-in reading chair or an old pair of slippers.

Now his quiet and his routines both were interrupted by the curiosity-seekers and looky-loos. It'd gotten to the point where he had to keep all his curtains drawn shut, and he missed the warmth of the morning sun in his breakfast nook as he drank his coffee and worked on his crossword puzzles.

He tried addressing the people outside directly, appealing to their better nature, but found himself the subject of too many photos in return and had to beat a hasty retreat back to the house. The experience had unsettled him greatly. He began imagining things escalating, the looky-loos getting bolder, beginning to trespass. What if they broke into his home? Took his things for souvenirs? Something had to change, and so, reluctantly, he decided to speak to the police.

The Muffin Man felt silly, as if he was play-acting being some kind of an undercover agent, dressing up in the long-forgotten clothes from the back of his closet and sneaking out through the back alley, but needs must, he told himself, needs must.

He was an upright citizen, full of fiber, moral and otherwise. He deserved to be left in peace.

The Muffin Man walked briskly and arrived at his destination quickly. There was no wait, atypical for a municipal building, and he was ushered right in, by Miss Dough, the receptionist, a middle-aged woman with a bouffant hairdo and a sour expression.

The sheriff was polishing the desk plate with his name on it—dark wood with a metal face and engraved lettering that spelled S. Trudel above the job title. The Muffin Man wondered why not use the full first name. There was certainly space for it. Was it a matter of economy? Governmental budget cuts?

In the few dealings he'd had with Sam Trudel over the years, the man had proven himself decent if a bit flaky. He had that very specific local politician appeal; his election advertisements usually did some take on "As Down-Home As Apple Pie."

The two of them made small talk. The office was oven-warm, making the Muffin Man sweat in his spy cosplay outfit, but one had to mind their manners and not rush into things, especially when asking for help.

"So, what brings you here today?" S. Trudel finally asked.

"It's those people." The Muffin Man sighed. "They are outside of my house day and night. Taking photos, trying to talk to me."

"You're a famous fella," the Sheriff noted good-naturedly.

"I don't want it," said the Muffin Man. "I need them to go away. They are adversely affecting the quality of my life." He was quite proud of that last sentence, having practiced it on the way over.

Sheriff Trudel composed his expression into seriousness. "Now, are they *on* your property?"

"Well, no. They stay outside."

"So, no trespassing then?"

"No, not as such." The Muffin Man could feel the beads of perspiration forming on his brow. "But it still feels very invasive."

"I can imagine," Sheriff S. Trudel said amicably. "I sympathize. I do. Just want to get all the facts straight. Are they blocking the street traffic?"

"Not the way Drury Lane is laid out."

"Okay, okay." Trudel nodded thoughtfully. "Have you tried asking them to leave?"

"Of course, I did," the Muffin Man exclaimed. Then, noting the traces of dramatic exasperation in his voice, adjusted his tone. "I asked, and they did not respect my wishes. I think, perhaps, if someone in the position of authority would ask..." He let the sentence trail off toward Trudel like a smoke signal.

"Okay, okay," the sheriff repeated. "Here's what we'll do. You go home and try to relax, and I'll come talk to them and ask them to disperse."

The Muffin Man was amazed that had worked. It was a technique he stole from his wife, ex-wife, who used to always say the best way to get someone to do something is making it seem like it's their idea.

"Thank you, Sheriff Trudel. That would be great."

"Call me Sam, please. And of course. We're here to help." The man smiled munificently as if expecting praise or signaling the end of the conversation or both.

The Muffin Man stood up. The old-fashioned vinyl reception chair released him with an unbecoming squeal. "So, when do you think you might come by?" he asked.

"Oh, I was thinking Friday or so."

It was Tuesday. The Muffin Man raised his eyebrows in what he hoped was a tactful manner.

The sheriff made a show of flipping through his planner. "You know what? It looks like I got some time tomorrow. Why don't I swing by then?"

"That would be great. Thank you."

"My pleasure," Sam Trudel boomed, offering a hearty handshake. "Don't you worry. We'll take care of this for you. Your privacy is valued here, Mr. Man."

Mr. Man. No one had referred to him as such in a long time. Back when he worked in an office, and the kids were in school, he was Mr. Man to a lot of folks. Now he freelanced from home, the kids turned into adults, and he became... well, a local curiosity, it seemed. Though, hopefully, not for long.

Sheriff S. Trudel wasn't the sternest of law enforcers—more Mr. Rogers than Judge Dredd—but he had to have been doing something right because he kept on getting re-elected.

The Muffin Man chose to trust in the law. That night, in his favorite recliner, with a mug of warm milk by his side, as he dozed intermittently to a crime show on TV, he let himself believe in the return of his perfectly quiet, perfectly anonymous semi-retirement. He dozed off with a smile on his face. It was lovely, especially considering the rude awakening life had in store for him.

TWO

The Muffin Man woke up to screaming. It took a moment to realize that's what it was, and another, longer one, to note that it was coming from the outside. He swung his comfortably rounded body into a sitting position, rubbed his sleep-crumpled face with his hands, and stuck his feet in his slippers.

The clock read 6:51 a.m. Much too early for such a disagreeable wake-up call. Inconceivable on a street as lovely as Drury Lane. And yet the scream sounded vaguely familiar, especially now that it was getting an accompaniment of sharp barks.

He shuffled to the living room window and pulled back the curtain. Daylight in all of its fresh-out-of-the-oven brightness assaulted his eyes. Squinting, he peered outside. Sure enough, there she was, Mrs. Cupcake—Vani Cupcake, she never went by Vanilla in all the years he had known her—screaming her perfectly coiffed head off. The miniature poodle by her side was going crazy, too. The Cupcakes had either bought the exact same dog every decade or cloned the original. The Muffin Man could never tell them apart or remember their names.

The dog wasn't what drew his focus anyway. That dubious honor belonged to the dead body that lay at Vani's feet. The juxtaposition of her blindingly white tennis shoes and red blood looked surreal in the morning sunshine.

The Muffin Man took in a deep breath and slowly released it. And here he thought the looky-loos were going to be his biggest problem. But no, the world always managed to surprise. And seldom pleasantly, he reflected, the older he got.

No choice now, though. He walked to the foyer, exchanged his slippers for moccasins, put a windbreaker over his pajamas, and stepped outside.

He wasn't the only one Vani's screams had summoned. Drury Lane was being stirred up whether it liked it or not. People were coming outside, sleepily, their expressions swiftly changing from confusion to horror. The talk swirled all around, all the typical things one might say in a situation like this. The what and why and who and did anyone see anything? How soundly they were sleeping. How shocked they were.

At least somebody had the presence of mind to call the emergency line. The Muffin Man wished it were him, but he was too busy convincing himself this wasn't all a terrible nightmare brought on by watching murder on TV before bed, and he was going to wake up from it any minute now.

There was a collective sigh of relief once the sirens dopplered closer, and then the car doors were being slammed, and the uniforms were among them.

"Mr. Man. Seeing you rather sooner than planned and what terrible circumstances." Sheriff Trudel had to be a morning person. No one looked that well put-together and alert at 7 a.m. He wore a light brown trench coat and a somber expression. "What happened here?" he asked as if the Muffin Man had any idea how a dead body of a stranger came to reside in the slightly overgrown, dewy grass of his front yard.

"I have no idea," was the honest response he got.

Everyone said the same thing. No one had any idea. Vani Cupcake had calmed down by now with her husband R.V.'s meaty arm around her shoulders.

Trudel went to ask her some questions.

"Talk to me, Sheriff," R.V. cut in. "My wife is clearly in shock."

The Cupcakes were a well-to-do local couple, fully enjoying Red's sudden stroke of luck some years back when a random inheritance from a distant relative paid for a Cinderella-like makeover of their entire life. It had made them as haughty and bristly as most parvenus.

"I get it, Red Velvet, and I apologize, but Vani here is our only material witness," Trudel explained in a reasonable tone. "She discovered the body. She may have seen something or someone."

Red harrumphed and tightened his hold on Vani's shoulders. But she didn't know any more than the rest of them. She was taking Sprinkles—that was his name, the Muffin Man remembered—for his 6:30 morning walk as always. She only walked as far as his house in the mornings, since the rest of the time there were always strangers loitering out front. And then she spotted the body.

No, she did not see anyone else. No, she did not hear anything suspicious. It was a perfect morning, really, until...

One by one people were interviewed and allowed to leave. Back they went to their comfortable houses and comfortable lives, with their home, Drury Lane, forever shadowed now. Forever marred.

The crime scene officers were wrapping up, too. The body was already loaded onto a stretcher, poised to be wheeled away for proper examination. It was no one anybody had recognized. A tall man with plain, even features and fair hair. Not that the Muffin Man looked all that closely.

"Mind if we go inside and have a chat, Mr. Man?" asked Sam Trudel after everyone left. The front yard was now cordoned off; wrapped in police tape and made to look like the most unwelcome of gifts.

He almost said "Call me Bran" but didn't, settling for a resigned nod instead.

"I'm having a deputy come by and watch the property for any of your unwanted visitors," Trudel told him, settling his long body down on the living room sofa. The middle-age doldrums seemed to have spared his form: no muscles rippled beneath his clothes, but he slayed uniformly flat with no gut or general sagginess that years bring.

The Muffin Man found the occurrence of the observation odd, considering, and pushed it away. He lowered his own rotund shape into his beloved recliner. They both still wore street shoes, he noted, making a mental note to clean the floors later. Funny what the brain picked up on in moments like these.

"So, last we spoke, you were complaining about all the people showing up near your house," Trudel began, after politely declining the offer of tea, opting for a glass of water instead. "You seemed... upset."

"Of course I was upset." The Muffin Man bristled before catching himself. "It's an upsetting sort of thing," he added sensibly.

The sheriff nodded his head sympathetically. His hair was styled, the Muffin Man noticed, the natural curl tamed with some sort of shiny mousse or gel. "You understand, Mr. Man, I have to ask... just how upset were you?"

"Meaning?" The Muffin Man did not like the question or the tone it was asked in.

"Well, in my experience upset people sometimes do the sort of things they normally wouldn't. Sometimes—" Trudel paused and sipped his water. "—very bad things."

"You think I..." It was unfathomable to even contemplate. The sentence was left hanging like an unfinished sandwich.

"I think there is a world where a man comes home exhausted after weeks of dealing with strangers interrupting his peaceful existence, gets pushed too far by one of the said strangers—asking for autographs or photos or some such nonsense—and just snaps." Trudel snapped his fingers to punctuate the last word for a truly unsettling effect. "You remember Ginger?"

Everybody remembered Ginger. She was one of their town's most memorable denizens. A lovely lady, the local librarian no less, sweet as could be, always smelling of cinnamon and cloves. One day she murdered her husband and his entire family, redefining Thanksgiving forever. When asked why, she simply said, "They had to go." When encouraged to elaborate, she offered the following, "Duncan and his clan, they made me feel like I was disintegrating, you know. Becoming less and less of myself. I had to put a stop to it."

She sounded perfectly sane, too, making the plea of temporary insanity a reach too far. The case made the news all over the world, screaming of domestic bliss gone terribly wrong, one catchy headline at the time.

"I didn't snap," The Muffin Man said in his most reasonable voice. "I have never lifted a hand to anyone in anger. And I never saw that man in my life. Before today."

"Okay, okay." Sam Trudel held up his spread hands palms up. "Just had to check. You know how it is."

The Muffin Man did. He watched enough crime shows. But it still left a bad taste in his mouth.

The silence that followed could not be described as comfortable.

"Well, I'll be off," the sheriff said, getting up. He placed his now empty glass on the small side table, neatly squaring it on the coaster, and offered his hand.

Mr. Muffin Man eyed it for a moment too long, then shook it reluctantly.

"Just doing my job," Trudel reiterated chummily. "No hard feelings."

"Right, yes."

"Well, I'll be off now," he repeated. "Come down to the station in the next day or two so we can take the official statement, if you would be so kind. And do not hesitate to reach out if you think of anything else."

The Muffin Man nodded. He saw the sheriff to the door and watched him walk to his car. The deputy was already there, juggling the early rising looky-loos on the scene. If they were interested in the house and his owner before, imagine what the police tape would do. He shook his head. All this notoriety and for what? He hadn't done anything worthy of notice in years. Decades.

He'd left fame, the strange fleeting thing that it was, firmly in his rearview mirror. From that perspective, it looked more like infamy. The Muffin Man had been a humble junior accountant just starting out in a large, prestigious firm when he uncovered what had since become universally known as the Soggy Bottom conspiracy. He didn't mean to blow the whistle, wasn't even sure he had it in him, but one thing led to another—the brashness of youth had never been a good advisor—and next he knew he was testifying. Hand raised, sworn in, the works.

The Soggy Bottom discovery had revolutionized the entire system for those who cooked the books and those who caught them, and he became the classic underdog hero, with his everyman appeal and shy charm. There were interviews and articles, photo ops and magazine profiles. None of it had ever sat right with him, and he was glad to leave it all behind, once the hoopla had died down.

The one good thing that came out of it was meeting his wife. Ex-wife, now. She was one of his interviewers—the sharpest one, for his money. The prettiest one, too. He couldn't believe she said yes, when finally, emboldened by all the attention, he had managed to ask her out. The vague disbelief in his good fortune, the surrealness of it all, had carried throughout their marriage, fading over the years but never dissipating entirely.

Cherry was always smart and a looker too, but for some reason, her career had never quite taken off beyond the local radius. Over time, it had soured her. Ready to put the disappointment behind her, she gave up her maiden name, Tart, for his without thinking twice. Though, he was pretty sure she was back to using it now.

There were good times, of course. Lots of them. They were happy once. That's what the Muffin Man chose to focus on whenever nostalgia yanked his chain. The way Cherry looked on the dance floor, the wild messes she made while cooking dishes he'd never heard of, the way she was with the kids, her eyes when she said she loved him.

She was glad to retire to be a housewife back then, he figured. It was a graceful exit from a dead-end career. Maybe he had read it all wrong. Maybe

Cherry missed it, missed the excitement. Maybe that's what being with Baguette, younger, accented, and charming, was all about.

She will hear of this, the Muffin Man knew. She'll recognize the front yard of the house she had spent most of her life in that had become a scene of a crime. Will she reach out? Their split was amicable, but agreeing to be friends and actually being friends with your ex were two very different things. Whenever they talked these days, it was all about the kids.

Cherry had been kind enough to leave him the house, knowing how much it meant to him. The place had been in his family for generations. She left a lot of things behind, and the ones she took were often random, parts of sets, etc., packing like someone in a hurry for a new life to begin.

Baguette owned one of the new, flashy builds on the other side of town, and she moved in with him. A happy ending, as far as divorces went.

The Muffin Man sighed. He didn't know why he was thinking of Cherry now. There were, after all, so many more pressing things to think about.

He peered outside once more, noting the people gathering there, then he retreated and shut the door firmly behind him. The house felt off to him somehow, ever since he first stepped back in, after the body and everything. There was a barely perceptible shift, like someone had been there in his absence. Did he lock the door after he left, when he first heard Vani's screams? He didn't think so. Were there any looky-loos around then? Did someone sneak in and out while he was distracted by the murder in his front yard?

The Muffin Man shook his head. That was how paranoia set in, he told himself, and he wouldn't let it —he had enough to deal with. He was simply and understandably upset and discombobulated by recent events. There'd been no one inside his home but him and the police.

Still, he took a good long look around the house to make sure all was as it should be, and nothing was missing. Everything was in order. Or course, it was. He felt calmed and ridiculous at the same time. Another head shake. No fool like an old fool.

He sighed, slowly exhaling the negative thoughts. His brain felt shrunken like a raisin—it would take at least two mugs of something strong and hot to revive it. But first things first.

The Muffin Man checked to make sure the curtains were drawn, then put a record on to block out some of the noise rising outside and set off to Swiffer the floors.

THREE

Sheriff Sam Trudel was not happy. He wasn't thrilled being woken up at the crack of dawn and forced to schlep to a crime scene, and he certainly wasn't crazy about having a murder in his town.

He'd been feeling a slowdown lately, now that retirement loomed more definitively ahead. Before, when the distance could still be measured in decades, he'd be excited to have his mettle tested. He still remembered the thrill of solving the Ginger murders.

Now he would have preferred to stay in bed. He got tired easier these days. The sheer effort of being an elected public official rode heavier on his shoulders. At the end of each day, his face drooped, the muscles slackening after holding up a jolly smile for so many hours.

And did it have to happen to the Muffin Man of all people? The town's once most illustrious person and lately just... a sour puss. Sure, going through a divorce improved no one's disposition, but Sam's wife assured him that according to the gossip vine the separation had been amicable. So what was it then? The man just did not seem happy. Never even offered his first name to go by, so it was still Mr. Man this and Mr. Man that, after all these years.

As far as Sam could tell the guy had a good life, all things considered. A brush with fame, a solid career, two good kids, a nice house, a hot number of a wife for a time, way out of his league, a comfortable semi-retirement. But no, some people were just never satisfied.

What's a few tourists gawking from the street? Harmless, really. But no, he had to go complain about it.

Now, of course, it was a nightmare. Whoever came up with that stupid nursery rhyme ought to be drawn and quartered. Did people have nothing better to do?

The Soggy Bottom thing was ages ago, why rehash it?

Sam spent the entire day interviewing the people of Drury Lane. What a bunch of fruitcakes, even if some of them did assure him they voted for him.

From the DeLeches who took a wild offense to him wanting to speak with their son—like Flan wasn't freshly out of prison, paroled out early for a bank robbery, and therefore the only person on the street with a proper rap sheet—to the Napoleon clan with their exhausting inferiority complexes to that former ballerina Pavlova and her unbearably depressive aura.

None of them of course knew anything. Nor did any of their neighbors.

The Cupcakes were no help. Vani was traumatized, though she claimed Sprinkles had suffered the worst of it. R.V. hovered over them as protective as an oversized shield.

No one was saying anything important, but somebody had to have known something, seen something. It was a small street in a small town. People knew each other beyond your usual curtain twitching and clandestine spying.

At least that's what he kept telling himself because a localized, contained murder was one thing—a manageable, solvable thing. But outside of that loomed a distinct and infinitely more dangerous possibility of this being something bigger, a part of a larger world encroaching into his quiet corner. And that made Sam very, very unhappy.

"I heard." A pair of soft arms wrapped around him, a kiss landed on his head. The smell of apricots and chocolate enveloped him. "I'm sorry."

Sam turned around and wrapped Ruggie in his arms. He really did have the best wife. Holding her felt like a homecoming, every time. If she ever walked out on him the way Cherry did on the Muffin Man, Sam didn't know what he would do.

His mother had always told him to marry a nice Jewish girl. With Rugelach, he figured he overshot. Still couldn't believe his luck.

She sat down next to him on the couch.

"It's a..." He waved his hand in the air nebulously, settling for, "It sucks."

"No one's talking?"

"Everyone's talking, and no one is saying anything I can use."

"What about the DeLeche kid?"

Ruggie never ceased to amaze him. She had a memory on her that could rival the police database.

"Oh, you know, the usual. He says he served his time, paid his debt to society, all that. His family was adamant that any undue attention to them would be reported as race-based discrimination."

"They did not!"

Sam rubbed his chin. A flake drifted down from the emergent stubble, making him wonder how long it had been there. He hoped not the entire time since lunch. But then he couldn't for the life of him remember if he had stopped for lunch at all. It had been that kind of a day.

"They did too. I must tread carefully. The eyes of the community are upon me. All that nonsense."

"Some people." Ruggie shook her head, making her dark curls bounce around her shoulders. "What, did they forget that their son had robbed the largest bank in town seven years ago?"

Sam shrugged. "You know how people are when it comes to families. The DeLeches especially."

"Dulce, their middle kid, is a sweetheart. I had her a few years back in my class. Such a nice girl."

"Well, that's one kid they got right," Sam huffed. The DeLeches' youngest, Tres, was already difficult, troubled, showing every sign of following in his brother's footsteps.

"They never found the money, did they?" Ruggie said like it wasn't really a question.

"Everyone figured Flan's partner, the one who never got caught, must have stashed it somewhere."

She arched her eyebrow. "Well, now that Flan's out, that's a reckoning waiting to happen, isn't it?"

Sam sighed heavily. "I just wanted a nice and easy ride into the sunset, you know."

"I know, hon." His wife snuggled up closer. They'd been discussing life after retirement. Maybe doing some traveling. The sheriff terms were long in their town, and they were considering making this be Sam's last one. Or at least, the one before last.

He shook his head. "What am I going to do, love?"

"What you always do," she replied reassuringly. "Succeed."

He used to think he'd still be a humble, low-ranking public servant if not for Ruggie's gentle yet firm push. She believed in him before he ever did, seeing the future Sam Trudel take shape years before it came true.

"Now come on," she said, rising off the couch and taking his hand. "I've got something to take your mind off your mind."

Sam felt a slow smile spread across his face from ear to ear. His lovely, prim and proper schoolteacher wife was as deliciously twisted in all the right ways as her name suggested. Happily, he followed her into the bedroom.

FOUR

Flan DeLeche wasn't happy because his family had been riding his ass ever since he got home, asking too many questions, and he no longer cared how well-meaning their interest was. He'd had enough.

For seven long years behind bars, freedom was all he could think of, all that got him from one endless day to the next. That and the money.

The money haunted him. He held it in his hands only once, more cash than most people see in their lifetime. A genuinely game-changing amount of dough. He watched his partner-in-crime walk away with it all, leaving him nothing but promises.

The promises were good. Navigating the dark waters of the prison system—the stygian gloom of oceanic trenches and depths untold—offered nothing else to hold on to, so Flan clutched to those promises like buoys, clinging on for dear life.

He could have squealed, of course, Got a reduced sentence, sure. But then what? He'd still get locked up, and though the release could've come out a few years sooner, he'd have nothing to return to. He'd be just another ex-con trying to get by.

Keeping silent earned Flan a chance at something more. A life better than any DeLeche in all their low middle-class splendor had ever had.

All he had to do was trust. A seemingly impossible proposition for a guy who double-checked every bill for fear of getting ripped off, but one had to start somewhere.

Now that Flan was out, he'd been having the hardest time getting hold of his former partner. They spoke on the phone but had yet to meet in person. There was always some excuse or other. It was maddening.

The worst was when Flan got accused of impatience.

"Impatient," he screamed into the phone so loudly he heard his own voice echo. "Impatient. Me. Seven years I waited. Seven years. Do you have any idea what that was like? Don't you ever call me impatient."

That was the last time they spoke. His partner-in-crime never did appreciate confrontation. Flan was gearing up to just show up out of the blue, arriving at the threshold (wherever that might be, he'd have to figure the address out first) with that ready-to-deal game face on, but now this freaking murder on his block was throwing everything for a loop.

He was already half-convinced he'd been followed around by the local deputies to ensure he stayed on the straight and narrow, and now this.

He'd be their prime suspect, Flan knew. Despite having never been accused, let alone convicted, of any violent crime. Once a criminal, always a criminal to the buttery-soft denizens of Drury Lane. The entire town, really.

The way the sheriff spoke to him earlier still chafed him. How dared he? Seven years of paying the society back for all the ways he had wronged it, and still Flan was spoken to like a convict. Like he was the second coming of Ginger-what's her-name.

He *should* kill someone just to prove them right, but violence had always churned his stomach. It did him a great disservice in prison, his flesh was dimpled and raised with evidence of it, but in this bright outside world he was determined to make his way without resorting to fighting.

His former bank-robbing friend was the same way. Soft as a cloud. It's why they robbed the bank in the first place, waving fake guns in the air. They were willing to commit a crime for the right payout, but nothing too dangerous.

"Egos are the only thing that ought to ever be bruised," his friend used to say.

Were they even friends anymore? There had been no prison visits for obvious reasons, and seven years was a long time. Hearts and minds had been changed in less.

"Never mind all that," Flan told himself. He didn't need friends. His share of the money would buy him plenty. Preferably somewhere far, far away from Drury Lane.

He just needed the cops to sort out this murder nonsense. Funny that, Flan trusting the cops to do their job right.

They caught *him* easily enough, but he made a lot of mistakes. Most of his time in prison had been spent dwelling on those. Stupid mistakes a kid would make, born out of eagerness and inexperience. He liked to think he'd do everything differently now, but he couldn't be sure, and, frankly, hoped to never find out.

All he wanted to do was take his share of the money and head down south until there was nothing but sand beneath his feet and nothing but ocean in front of him as far as the eye could see. Start a new life and never look back.

The crazy thing was that one of these lazy, whitebread homeslices he had for neighbors might be a murderer.

Could it be the Muffin Man himself? It boggled the mind. Flan had known him for as long as he could remember. The guy was as mild-mannered and soft as they came. His wife was a hottie for an older woman. Flan used to fantasize about her. All those yummy curves. Whatever happened to her? They seemed happy enough around the time Flan got locked up, but now the Muffin Man was always alone.

And there had been all those nutters gathering around on the street outside his house, trying to catch a glimpse of him or snap a picture. Flan had to ask his parents what that was all about. Turned out it was something about an old conspiracy the Muffin Man uncovered way back when. Flan was surprised anyone still cared. But then people were like that, obsessed with all the wrong things.

He'd be glad to see the end of them. Hopefully now with the murder and all, the cops would shoo them away. Ever since his arrest, crowds gave Flan anxiety. First, the trial, then the prison. He'd breathe easier once everyone left him alone. He'd be perfectly happy on some barely inhabited island in the tropics, just him and a sexy older lady or two to take care of him.

He just had to get his money first.

FIVE

When the shouting from the street got too loud, the Muffin Man put music on. Nothing racy, just Cake, but he turned up the volume until it was all he could hear.

It wasn't just the looky-loos outside anymore. The press was there now, too. Vultures, all of them.

The band blared "You're Never There" on the stereo, and he wished it were true. He wished he was left alone. It would only get worse now, he reasoned. Unless S. Trudel does his job and quickly.

The Muffin Man had some work to do but, try as he might, he could not concentrate on the figures in front of him. When he closed his eyes, he could still see the dead body on his lawn. All that blood.

He hadn't mowed the grass in much too long. Without Cherry to make him, the act seemed futile. The lawnmower had been acting up for years, and he couldn't find the motivation to fight with the machine for something as arbitrary as yard upkeep. If the neighbors had a problem with it, he figured they'd say something. Or they'd glare the message at him the way Pavlova tended to. She always acted like she had a stick up her bum, but then again, it could have just been her ballerina posture, holding strong after all these years. He'd never seen her perform, but Cherry had once, a long time ago, and said the woman seemed light as air. A funny quality for someone with such heavy gravitas.

Now the Muffin Man supposed he wouldn't be allowed to mow the lawn even if he wanted to. Preservation of the crime scene and all that.

It troubled him to think that a murder could be slept through like that. That a murderer could lurk right outside your windows, and you'd never know.

The music was getting annoying. He liked it well enough normally but wasn't used to listening to it on such deafeningly high volume.

He switched over to television. Watching a crime show now seemed wrong so he opted for a nature program. It put him to sleep within twenty minutes the way those types of things always did.

In his dream, there was a heavy burning smell. He was trying and failing to get to the oven. When he finally did, all he could see was a baking sheet on fire with charred figures writhing on it. The Muffin Man woke up panting and gasping like a rescued drowning victim. His shirt was clammy with sweat.

It was still daytime, though most of the light was dulled by the tightly drawn curtains. Elephants majestically roamed the African savanna on TV. They didn't seem to have a care in the world, but the Muffin Man knew better. He'd seen enough nature shows to have a working knowledge of the climate change challenges and poaching dangers. The predators, it seemed, were everywhere, just waiting for a chance to pounce.

He got up and stretched. His weary bones sounded like castanets. He was too old to sleep anywhere but his bed with its ergonomic mattress.

Switching the TV off, he walked into the kitchen. He should have left it alone, but he just had to see. A mere glimpse of the chaos outside.

"The Muffin Man," people outside screamed the moment they saw his window curtain twitch. "What do you know about the murder? Do you have any suspects in mind? What are your thoughts? Do you think it has anything to do with Soggy Bottom?"

He backed away from the window as if he'd been scalded and shuddered. He was right—it was so much worse now. The curiosity seekers had turned aggressive, and the aggressive-by-nature press was only spurring them on.

The deputy outside was doing a half-decent job of keeping them off his lawn, if not keeping them quiet. It wasn't enough.

The Muffin Man went back to the living room and sank into the too-soft, old recliner, cradling his head with his hands firmly pressed against his ears.

This, he thought grimly, would be his go-to pose for the next who knew how long. His survival mode. Hopefully there was enough food in the kitchen to last, though eating at the moment seemed like an impossible proposition. Maybe some more music.

Riffling through his record collection, he settled on an odd choice. Bread, a real seventies throwback. Once upon a time, he and Cherry used to dance to those corny love songs. Alas, it wasn't the sort of music one could blast, and thus didn't help much in blocking out the outside noise.

He went and found his noise-canceling headphones, slapped the unwieldy giant earmuff-like things on his ears, and sighed. The newfound silence had a peculiar undercurrent of tension beneath it, as though at any moment the sound could break through. Still, it was better than nothing.

The Muffin Man grabbed a pencil, got out his crossword puzzle book, turned to a fresh page, and began solving the clues. The rhythm of inputting answers into the tiny squares in blocky print letters always had the calming effect he craved.

Outside, gathering like storm clouds, people shouted his name.

SIX

"Detective Cotta," Sherrif Trudel said, infusing his voice and his handshake with false bonhomie. "We're pleased to have you here."

"Call me Panna," the woman replied with a heavy Italian accent. She had a perfect milky complexion at odds with her heavy brows and serious dark eyes and wore a white suit so crisp it didn't seem real.

How did people wear things like that outside of TV? he wondered. How'd they keep it clean?

She didn't look like a detective. Sam wasn't sure what she looked like. Maybe some kind of business barracuda?

And no, he wasn't pleased to have her there. It felt patronizing, like no one trusted the local yokel to solve the case. But then again, it did take some pressure off his shoulders.

The rest of his team regarded Detective Cotta with a mixture of curiosity and distrust. This was, after all, the first time Interpol had come to town.

"May I address the room?" she asked Trudel.

"Of course." He made the universal "be my guest" gesture, pleased she had thought to ask. "Go right ahead."

"Thank you, Sheriff." She turned with an oddly avian grace. "As you likely know by now, my name is Detective Cotta. I work for Interpol, and my involvement here has to do with the victim of the recent murder on Drury Lane."

"We solved the Ginger murders just fine on our own," piped in the deputy in the back.

Sam Trudel rolled his eyes inwardly.

Cotta seemed unfazed. "Yes, well, be that as it may, this murder involves a foreign national, thus the Interpol's interest."

"What nationality is the victim?" the voice from the back continued.

"Danish."

"Ah."

"And your name?" Detective Cotta squinted at the deputy.

"Pastry. Paul. Call me Puff. Everybody does."

"Officer Pastry," Cotta said in a scalpel-like tone. "Your cooperation is most appreciated."

Puff blushed. A terrible trait for a man, worse for a policeman, Trudel thought.   Puff was a brash redhead who sometimes spoke before he thought things through, but his dedication to the job was unparalleled. Sam often had to tell him to go home at the end of his shift.

For the past few days, Puff was one of the deputies posted to the Muffin Man's house to keep the madness and the media at bay. He wasn't the most effective—that honor went to deputy Linzer. A shoo-in for the position of second-in-command, Linzer was a stern and somber Austrian transplant who lived and breathed crime and spent entirely too much time at the gym, but Puff was the most enthusiastic, working the longest shifts without so much as a word of complaint.

The looky-loos never left. There was just something about this case. Sam even had the deputies deliver food to the Man residence. There was no way for the Muffin Man to go get it himself at the store. As far as Sam knew, the man hadn't left the house in all this time.

It had to be awful, sitting there all alone, Sam thought, with both your peace of mind and privacy crudely ripped away. He sympathized while keeping in mind this could be a potential suspect.

"So then, why was a Danish national found dead on Drury Lane?" Detective Cotta looked around the room. "Any ideas?"

"The Muffin Man," said Linzer.

"The Muffin Man?"

"The Muffin Man."

"What about him?"

"He's been a point of focus lately in the community," Linzer explained. "Ever since someone leaked his address to the general population. I presume you are familiar with the Soggy Bottom case?"

Cotta gave a sharp nod.

'Well, the victim—" Linzer consulted his notes. "—Mr. Remonce, he was found on the Muffin Man's lawn. There could be a connection."

Cotta nodded again, softer and more thoughtfully this time. "The Soggy Bottom case, that was decades ago, no?"

"Thirty years to the day of the murder," Puff threw in. "I checked," he added.

"That's good work," Sam said, sending Puff beaming with pride.

"An anniversary murder," Detective Cotta mused, tapping a long, elegant finger to her chin. Her accent made a staccato symphony out of every sentence.

"You think it's possible?" S. Trudel asked.

"At this point of the investigation, I'm not ruling anything out." She picked a piece of invisible lint from her pristine lapel. "I'd be most interested in speaking to this Mr. Man."

"That I can arrange," Sam said, relieved at having an easily achievable task to perform.

The Muffin Man looked worse and worse every time Trudel saw him. He couldn't blame the guy either, not with everything that was going on all around him.

They were let into his house with a sigh and downtrodden resignation.

"Mr. Man," Sam boomed in his best elected-public-official voice. "Brought you some coffee and a guest."

The Muffin Man was wearing a pair of gingham pajamas with the top buttoned all wrong. His normally robust complexion looked pale and waxy.

"Call me Bran," he said by way of thanks, taking the coffee and gulping down seemingly half of it.

"Bran," Sam repeated, brightening up. This was the first time the man had offered up his first name. Ideally, it meant that a kind of camaraderie had been achieved, however forced, but under the circumstances, somehow it seemed more like an admission of defeat.

Sam Trudel would have almost preferred the other, more officious and standoffish version of the man to this broken-spirited one.

"Did we wake you?" Detective Cotta asked, looking around.

"No, no," he said softly, shifting from foot to foot. "I don't sleep much these days."

"I'm sure it hasn't been easy," Cotta said briskly, like someone eager to dismiss with pleasantries and get to the meat of things. "Do you know a Mr. Remonce? Niels Remonce?"

The Muffin Man shook his head, then verbalized the no.

"You don't recall his name in connection with the Soggy Bottom case?"

The man stood silent.

"Bran," Sam prodded gently.

The Muffin Man pushed his hands into his hair and shook his head again. "That was decades ago."

"Three decades to be precise. To the date of the murder."

"Really?" He seemed surprised.

"Really."

"Still no. Doesn't ring a bell. What kind of name is that, anyway?"

"Danish."

"Ah." He sipped his coffee some more.

'I'd like to discuss the details of the Soggy Bottom case with you," Cotta said.

The Muffin Man shuffled into the living room, gesturing for them to follow. They sat themselves on the sofa, while he took the recliner, turning it to face his guests.

"All the details are a matter of public record," Bran said tiredly. "You don't need me."

"Still, I'd very much like to hear it from you," Cotta insisted.

Sighing like a punctured balloon, the Muffin Man finished his coffee. Crumbling the empty cup in his hands, he proceeded to tell his story.

"Once upon a time, a bright-eyed and bushy-tailed accountant fresh out of school landed a coveted position in a large, prestigious firm. He was determined to climb the ladder by working the hardest and putting in the longest hours. He completed the assignments given to him and went looking for more. Extracurricular work, he thought, was the thing to impress the powers that be. Only he found something that wasn't meant to be seen. A dirty secret at the heart of the entire company. A book cooking, money laundering operation of gargantuan proportions, clever and audacious enough to go on for years, hidden in the shadows. The more he dug, the more he uncovered. And if it was just about money, he might have hesitated, worried about what speaking out might do. But he kept coming across dismissed lawsuits from people affected—*ruined*—by the company, and he realized he had to say something, do something. So he reached out to the appropriate authorities and blew the whistle as loud as he knew how. The investigation ensued. Arrests were made. The company shut down. The case went to trial. Etcetera. etcetera. The rest is history."

The Muffin Man said it all in one breath, like he'd done it many times before, exhaling loudly once finished.

"You know what I'm hearing the loudest?" Detective Cotta asked after a beat.

"What?"

"I'm hearing a lot of lives ruined. People who worked for the company, people who were victimized by them."

Sheriff Trudel nodded along, seeing where Cotta was going.

"I'm wondering if any of them might have been named Remonce," she mused aloud, without taking her eyes off of Bran.

The Muffin Man scratched his unshaven chin. "As I said, I've never heard that name."

"We'll check it out," Sam reassured her.

"Did anyone stand out to you from that time?" Cotta asked Bran. "Anyone particularly vindictive or vicious?"

"Honestly, it all felt kind of like a nightmare. It still does when I look back, so I try not to. I mean, yes, a lot of people were upset, naturally. But it's been thirty years." He shook his head as if in disbelief over the passage of time, repeating, "Thirty years."

Detective Cotta inclined her head in a way that could have taken for sympathy, erroneously. "And this recent situation with the spectators. You were very upset, yes? Came to speak to the sheriff. Any signs of violence outside ever, among the onlookers?"

"No." Bran shook his head. "I mean, I wasn't paying that much attention to them. I tried not to, but no. They were annoying but peaceful."

"This is the photo of the victim. Do you recognize him at all?"

Bran stared at the image of a blandly handsome, Scandinavian-looking man. It was the first time he was seeing him without all the blood. "No, sorry."

"Very well. Thank you." Cotta put the photo away. "Have you received any threats prior to the murder? Any knowledge of anyone who might have wished you harm? Anyone you might have wished harm to?"

Cotta shifted gears like an Italian race car: precisely and dispassionately. Sam thought he would hate to be on the receiving end of her inquiries.

Bran stood up. "Look, Detective," he said, balling his hands into fists and releasing them. "I'm a nobody. A divorcee. A semi-retired accountant. I had a brush with fame, so to speak, ages ago and left it there. In. The. Past. No one bothers with me on a normal day. I'm not that interesting. None of this makes any sense to me. It has upended my entire life. Things like these happen to somebodies. And like I said, I'm a..."

"But you're not a nobody," Cotta countered, narrowing her eyes. "You're the Muffin Man."

Deflated, he dropped back down into his recliner.

Cotta got up and began perusing the photos on the walls, then his bookshelves.

"A big mystery fan," she commented, nodding toward the spines of the books.

He shrugged. "Those mostly got left behind by my ex-wife and the kids after they moved out. I don't read as much as I'd like, I'm afraid."

"Thank you for your time," Cotta said, followed by Trudel's more sincere sentiments of similar nature. "We'll be in touch."

"How was he killed?" the Muffin Man asked, surprising himself.

"A very sharp knife met a very vulnerable artery." Cotta's mouth stretched sideways into something like a casual frown.

She really did have the most exquisite skin, the Muffin Man observed, as delicate as cooked cream. But it was not a friendly face.

"Lock that door, Mr. Man. Bran," the sheriff corrected himself. "Hopefully this'll all be over soon."

The Muffin Man nodded. He walked them to the small hallway, waiting out of sight line until they closed the door behind them. Then he stepped forward, reached out, and quickly engaged the locks.

There was a sour taste in his mouth, and his pajama top, he noticed, was buttoned all wrong. The indignities, big and small, just kept piling up.

SEVEN

"What do you mean next week?" Flan balled his hand so tightly into a fist that he could feel his nails digging bloody crescents into his palm. It was helping him to keep his temper under control, something he learned in prison. His other hand was holding the phone, knuckles white from tension.

"I mean, I am getting the money together," the familiar voice came through the line. "It is a lot of money. I didn't just bury a bag of cash in the backyard for seven years, you know. I moved things around. I invested."

"But I've been waiting and waiting." Flan cringed at the whiny note in his tone.

"And I appreciate that." The voice sounded so calm, imbued with quiet confidence. "I have been working on putting this together for you. Don't worry."

"Don't worry," Flan repeated quietly, pushing down the rising scream. "Don't worry. Why would I worry?"

"Exactly," the voice said, reasonably. "You have no reason to worry. If I wanted to stiff you, I would have left town, left the country years ago. I could have changed my name, my life. But I stayed here, waiting for you as promised."

Flan nodded along to the logic streaming from his phone. It was true, wasn't it? Everything he was hearing made sense.

"I would have had this all ready for you on time, but your early release threw me off a bit. No one's fault, these things happen. It's being taken care of. I mean it when I say you have nothing to worry about."

"Yeah, okay," Flan said, unballing his fist. The tiny cuts stung. "But like... are you even in town? I mean, you could be calling from anywhere and just like messing with me."

The voice tsked, then there was a clicking sound. A moment later a picture came through on Flan's phone. He recognized the main plaza, the fountain there fashioned after Hansel and Gretel. For a moment he thought about running there right now and catching his partner in the act, but what good would it do? It would only prove his para...

"Don't be paranoid," the voice cut in as if reading his thoughts. "Everything is on track. Just thread the water and hold on a bit more."

Flan looked outside his window. If the water metaphor was to be continued, outside it was red and full of fins. The hungry media, the paparazzi, the random vultures—the morbid tourism business was booming.

"Yeah, I'll hang on," he said into the phone. "One more week right?"

"If not sooner," the voice reassured him. "Start making plans."

Flan hung up thinking about the money. Plans, he already had. They swirled in his mind day and night.

He drew the curtain and went into the kitchen, letting his rumbling stomach guide his feet.

In prison he ate little, avoiding the unpalatable slop whenever possible; now he couldn't stop.

"Whatcha making, mama?"

Pan DeLeche turned around. Short and stout, she not only looked like the famous teapot but wore colorful blouses to play into the image.

"I'm thinking enchiladas tonight," she said, smiling. "Unless you want something else."

"Enchiladas sound good," he replied, nearly salivating at the thought of bubbling-hot cheese.

"Who were you talking to?" she asked, nosy as ever.

"A friend."

"Uh-huh," she said, loading it with suspicion. "Go help your father in the basement before he throws out his back again."

Flan grabbed a banana from the fruit bowl and descended the rickety stairs to discover Chu DeLeche trying to move a washing machine.

"What's up, padre?" he said through a mouthful of banana.

"The machine leaked. Trying to clean it up."

"Hang on." Flan finished the banana and discarded the peel into a small trash can full of dryer lint. "Mom's worried about your back."

Chu grunted.

Together they moved the machine and mopped up the spill with old towels, before pushing the washer back in place.

"Nice to have help around the house again, hijo." His father patted him on the shoulder.

Flan felt a stab of guilt the way he always did after every nice interaction with his parents. Soon enough it would get obliterated by one of their more typical cutting remarks, but right now, he let himself enjoy the nice.

"How's work, Dad?"

"Oh, you know, up and down, up and down." Churro's Chimneys had been in business ever since Flan could remember, and his father had always made the same joke. "At least, I get to be my own boss."

"Right, right."

Flan tensed, expecting a lecture on the importance of honest labor. The thing was, it didn't appeal to him back when he was a kid and didn't do the trick now. He had always wanted his money like he wanted his life like he wanted his women—easy.

"Had some kids leave me cookies and milk, like I'm Santa," his father said instead.

"Cute."

"What are you going to do now, hijo? Your mother and I worry, you know. At least tell me you have a plan."

"Yes," Flan said, relieved he didn't have to lie for a change. "I promise you I have a plan."

Afterward, in his room half-preserved like a mausoleum of his bygone youth, half-converted into a gym no one ever used, he sat on his childhood bed, narrow enough to uncomfortably remind him of prison bunks, and contemplated how strange it was to make plans in the world as unpredictable as this one. Despite having lived in this town his entire life, whenever Flan went outside, he felt like a stranger surrounded by strangers. It was like everyone was playing some elaborate game, and he was the only one not given the instructions. It made him sad, and occasionally very, very mad. Blood-boilingly mad. He learned to push it down because he was too small to fight, and now also because his parole officer was too tough to let things like that go. But every so often he just wanted to... well, that's what the pillows were for.

Flan hammered them with his fists and screamed into them until the heavy storms of his rage would pass, and he could see the blue skies again.

He had observed the same thing in his kid brother. It worried him, but what could he do? People were who they were. There was nothing to be done, nothing to be said to help. After all, nothing had ever helped him.

He thought the bank robbery would be his way out of all this. Another stupid, half-baked plan. Albeit one that could, perhaps, still be salvaged.

Flan had started his criminal career, if one could call it that, with break-ins. Picking locks had always come easy to him, not that in a neighborhood like his anyone had bothered locking up much. As a youth, he liked sneaking into people's places. There was just something about seeing their lives without them in it. Like walking through the empty movie sets before the actors arrive. Sometimes he didn't even take anything. Rearranging a few things to mess with the owners' minds was his signature move. Something about bringing a tiny measure of disorder to the proper and orderly Drury Lane pleased and amused him. He should have stuck with that, in retrospect. He was clearly not cut out for the life of crime... or punishment.

Flan looked around the room, noting the peeling wallpaper, the water-damage stain in the corner of the ceiling. Theirs had to be the shabbiest house on

Drury Lane. Maybe he'd leave his parents some of the money before he split. Half apology, half good-bye. He knew it couldn't have been easy having a son like him. The embarrassment alone...

Oh well. A new reputation couldn't be bought, but a new roof could. He'd start with that.

Dreaming of spending money he did not yet possess, Flan dozed off. He slept spottily, the way he always did, ever since the first year of prison when a particularly nasty cellmate had taught him extreme caution, and woke up to the sound of his mom calling his name, and the smell of enchiladas drifting through the house. For a moment, he time-traveled back to being a kid, before everything went wrong. And then life came crashing back, and he staggered down the stairs to eat his feelings until the comfortable numbness set in.

EIGHT

"He's older than he looks," Sheriff S. Trudel said, re-reading the freshly printed-out information about their victim. "Looked," he corrected himself.

"Indeed," Cotta said, sipping her espresso. She frowned at the paper cup. "Times like this I miss my partner."

"He'd solve this in a minute, huh?" Sam joked, trying to elevate the mood, more out of habit than necessity.

"No," Cotta replied icily. "But he'd make a proper espresso."

Wordless, Sam went back to the papers.

"So, a mild-mannered actuary enters the country for the first time, stating pleasure not business, gets killed three days later, and no one knows anything."

"Oh, someone knows something," Cotta said, finishing her distasteful espresso and tossing the cup into the bin with a professional basketballer's grace. "Three days is a long time. He talked to people, went places. Every contact leaves a trace, and all that."

"Right, right." Sam rubbed his forehead. "Did anyone contact his employer, landlord, neighbors?"

"Yep," Linzer spoke up. "Good people. All speak perfect English." He flipped open his notebook, peering at the scribbles that everyone but him found indecipherable. "Remonce was employed by the same company for twenty-six years. Never a problem. The neighbors said he was quiet and kept to himself."

"Like all the known serial killers," Puff interjected. Linzer shot him a withering glance.

"Remonce owned his apartment," he went on. "Was financially solvent. Did not have many friends, it seems. No spouse, no partner. However, one of his co-workers told me Remonce confided in him about dabbling in online dating."

"Who isn't?" Puff said, receiving another stern look.

Sam sighed. "Not much to go on."

"No, sir. So I dug deeper, and it turns out Remonce comes from money on his mother's side. Better still, his mother lost a fortune in the Soggy Bottom fiasco. She ended up drinking, going from rehab to rehab. There was a nasty divorce."

"But he was an adult by then, no?" Cotta asked.

"Seventeen."

"An impressionable age," Sam pointed out.

Cotta drummed her fingers on the desk's particleboard surface. She looked at Trudel, arching her eyebrows, her expression intense.

"So what, he waits thirty years to avenge his family? Comes after the Muffin Man and gets slain in the front yard?" Sam shook his head. "I don't buy it."

"You know what they say about serving up revenge," Cotta said.

"At any rate, Mr. Man would not know of Remonce. His mother used her maiden name, Schnecken," Lizer concluded, putting his notebook away.

"I'd change my name to Remonce, too, if I were her," Puff joked. No one laughed.

"So there is something like a motive, "Cotta summed up, rubbing her hands together.

"And an opportunity, I suppose," Sam offered.

"Time we took a closer look at the Muffin Man, no?"

Sam shrugged. "I just don't see him for it."

"It is such a polite mystery, is it not?" Detective Cotta brushed down her milky-white silk blouse. "These two nice middle-aged men. One a victim, one a suspect. A thirty-year-old connection. An old scandal swept under a rug. No one to say a bad word about either of them. The two of them are so perfectly—" She searched for the right word. "—milquetoast. No one saw anything, no one heard anything. It's like something out of Agatha Christie."

"I love Christie," Sam said. "My wife and I have read every single one of her books."

"Well, then." Cotta lifted her index finger as if to make a point. "You'll know to expect the unexpected."

"It can be anyone," Trudel agreed. "In theory." He had always liked that about all those wonderful old mysteries. The way no one was ever above suspicion. How the seemingly innocent could turn out to be the guiltiest of all. More often than not the endings surprised him. He wondered what that said about him as a detective.

"You think your small town is too quaint for such things, but..." Panna Cotta shook her head. "There is this saying. Everyone is kneaded out of the same dough but not baked in the same oven."

"Is that Italian?"

"Scottish, actually."

Sam thought about how much he liked it and hoped his mind would hold on to it. At least until he could share it with Ruggie, who had a memory like a steel vault.

Cotta thought about how much she missed her partner, who taught her that proverb among many other things. Interpol had viewed this as a single-person job and was probably right, but having Bis with her would make things so much easier. More interesting, too. He had a way of looking at the world differently than anyone she'd ever met. They were the proverbial odd couple when first partnered up. An older, seasoned detective and a young hotshot. A crusty old-timer and a smooth newcomer. Cotta and Cotti, even their names were like something out of a cop buddy comedy. But it worked, the two of them had balanced each other out perfectly.

Here, in this town, too cute and small for her liking, with their jolly sheriff and terrible espresso, she felt unmoored. All she wanted to do was solve the case and go home. The sooner the better.

International assignments looked good on a resume, but it wasn't all James Bond-style adventures. Not by a long shot.

Detective Cotta sighed as she brushed down a spotless sleeve. "Okay, then, the Muffin Man. Layer by layer. Let's see what we can find."

NINE

The cops were back, was his first thought upon hearing the knock on the door. No one else knocked. The deputies did not let anyone get that close. he pushed his anxiety away; maybe it was only them bringing some food.

The Muffin Man peered through the curtained window that offered a side view of the front porch. Oh... not cops at all.

He rushed to his bedroom and quickly changed out of his pajamas into the cleanest-looking pair of chinos and a shirt. A quick whiff test revealed a light yeasty smell, but nothing too terrible. He ran to the bathroom to wet his hair and pat it down. Then, making sure all was buttoned and zipped correctly, he unlocked the door and quickly stepped aside to get out of plain view.

"Come in."

He closed the door the second his guest was through.

"It's a madhouse out there," she said.

"Hi, Cherry." His heart gave an awkward lurch and sped up. Strange how after all these years, after all that's happened, she still had that effect on him.

"Hi, Bran," she said and smiled. It was such a nice smile. She took off her shoes without him having to ask and walked toward the living room. Through her nylon stockings, he could see her red toenail polish.

"How are you?" she asked, stopping by the couch, putting a hand on his shoulder, and looking so sincere that he wanted to tell her everything right then and there. Cry on her shoulder, wallow in self-pity, all that.

"I'm holding up," he replied instead, stoically. "Just waiting out the circus."

She nodded sympathetically. "You look good," she lied kindly. "Especially considering."

"You look great," he said back because she did, but it felt awkward the moment the words left this mouth. "How's Baguette?" he asked to cover up the gaffe. He didn't really want to know how Baguette was.

"He's good, same, you know." Cherry waved her hand in the air. "When was the last time you talked to the kids?"

"Um." He had to think. "It's been a few weeks, I guess. Before all of this. They are busy, so..."

"Sure, sure. But they do read the news, you know."

The Muffin Man wondered if the kids' phone calls were some of the ones he had ignored recently. He didn't mean to, but the phone simply got to be too much; he had to power it off.

"Shoot. Did you talk to them? What did they say?"

"You know, the usual. They are concerned. I reassured them everything is all right. Parenting is the same no matter what age they are, isn't it?" Cherry mused.

"They weren't too... upset?"

"No, no. They've got their own issues. Poppy has to find a new apartment."

"Again?"

"Oh, you know how she rolls. Besides, it's for the best. Her old neighborhood is really much too seedy for my liking."

He nodded, trying to remember if he had seen it. The girl moved around like a tumbleweed.

"And Berry?"

Cherry did a dramatic sigh. "Berliner thinks he might have gotten his girlfriend pregnant."

"Are you kidding me?" For a moment, Bran forgot about his own predicament. "We're going to be grandparents?"

"They are taking the very mature approach of not talking about it at the moment. But you know,

Berry, he's going to want to do the right thing. Whatever they decide that might be."

Bran felt a small buzz of pride at that. His son had good moral fiber, a real Man.

For a moment they looked at each other, then burst out laughing.

"I feel too young to be a grandmother."

"Same," he confessed.

"How are you really?" she asked after a while. "I care, you know."

He nodded, not trusting himself to speak.

"Okay. An easier question. When was the last time you ate something?"

He tried to remember.

She shook her head. "If you have to think about it, it's been too long. Come on."

They made their way into the kitchen, where Cherry proceeded to raid the fridge and cabinets, pulling out ingredients for a meal. She was always so good at that—making something out of nothing. She used to joke it was her only post-apocalyptic skill.

"What would I do?" he'd ask.

"I don't know. Hunt, I guess. Kill things."

"I'm not much of a killer," he'd say mock-ruefully.

"Yeah, we'd probably starve to death," she'd tell him and kiss him like it didn't matter. Those were the days.

"I miss this house sometimes," Cherry said, stirring something delicious smelling in the skillet.

"This old place? I thought Baguette had a brand-new everything."

"He does. But it's so, I don't know, sterile. No personality, no warmth. I try and try, but..." She trailed off and began sorting through the spices.

Bran searched for something to say.

"The detectives looked at the books in the living room. All those mysteries you and the kids had left behind. They thought they were mine. Probably figured that's where I get my ideas."

Cherry shook her head at the absurdity of it. "I've read all of them, and I'm pretty sure none have a murderer stupid enough to kill in his own front yard and leave the body there."

"You should tell them that," he joked.

The meal was simple but flavorful. The best he'd had in ages. They ate, engaging in surprisingly comfortable small talk.

"Is that a knock?"

Bran frowned. "I hope not."

"Thought I heard a knock."

"I'll go see," he offered. He did. There was no one at the door.

"I must be hearing things," Cherry said, rolling her eyes. "It is rather noisy outside. I don't know how you can stand it."

"I play music. Loudly."

"Oh yeah?" She smirked. "Anything good?"

"Sure. Bread. Remember Bread?"

She laughed, then began singing, "I wanna make it with you."

It tugged at his heartstrings all wrong. Did it show in his face? Because she stopped singing.

"I should go," she told him. "It's getting late."

"Stay," he wanted to say. But he was never good at words when it mattered. Not then, and certainly not now.

"Thank you for coming," he said instead. "This was the first nice evening I've had in a long time."

"I'm sorry." Cherry put her palm on his cheek. It felt as pleasantly refreshing as the other side of the pillow. He wished he had shaved. He wished he had known she was coming. The place was a mess. He was a mess. How it all must have looked to her. Like something she was happy to leave behind, he bet. "It'll all be all right," she said. And he closed his eyes briefly, letting the moment imprint upon his memory.

And then she was gone, and he was all alone again. It was like when you sit in the dark for a while, and someone comes and turns the lights on. After they shut them off and leave, the darkness is so much deeper. Impenetrable. Unfathomable. Like the universe before the Big Bang.

The Muffin Man sighed so deeply it might have passed for a cry. There were times when missing his old life hit him like a boxer's gloved fist, throwing him off balance, making him loose his footing. In his opinion, there was nothing worse for a man than helplessness. He didn't fight for Cherry back then, but in the years since he had promised himself that next time, should the opportunity arise, he would fight for what mattered, At any cost. Would kill for it if he had to. Such grand thoughts for such a small life. He sighed again, quieter now.

Then he found his bulky headphones and settled down on the couch to watch some old home movies.

TEN

The knock came the following day, and it was much too heavy and commanding sounding to imagine it could be Cherry again. Or anyone other than...

The Muffin Man opened the door and let the police in. He had stopped keeping up with their logistics and rankings—sheriff, detective, deputies, they were all the same: unhelpful and full of suspicion.

The Italian woman, in particular, made him feel like such a heel.

"Good morning, Bran," Sheriff Trudel boomed at him with out-of-place cheer. "Brought you a coffee."

He accepted it gratefully and took a sip. Somehow, it had just the right amount of milk.

Cotta nodded and did that thing with her mouth that didn't quite pass for a smile the way it was meant to. "Would you mind if we take a look around?"

"Do you have a warrant?"

She produced the paperwork. The Muffin Man experienced a distinct sinking stone sensation in the pit of his stomach just looking at it. Unreal. He felt like a man waking up from one nightmare into another, worse one. When would it end? He took a deep steadying breath.

"Your shoes," he said.

"What?"

"Take your shoes off if you're going to go all over the house."

She seemed amused as she kicked off her sensible white brogues. S. Trudel had to twist his body to follow suit. He then nodded to Linzer to do the same. In stocking feet, they padded around the Muffin Man's house.

Bran closed his eyes. Just when he thought he had no privacy left to violate.

The coffee had turned acidic in his mouth as he stood there, clutching the warrant. He went over to the couch and sat down.

A stick-your-head-in-the-oven desperation washed over him. He chewed his lip and waited until it was over.

They took his computer and several other things, all carefully bagged in plastic and labeled. He was given a receipt to add to the useless pile of paper accumulating to spell out his guilt. His doom.

"Thank you for your cooperation," Cotta said, slipping her surprisingly dainty feet back into her shoes. "We'll be in touch."

"Bran," Trudel added amicably. He was overusing his first name the way politicians and salesmen tended to. The Muffin Man wished things could go back to the way they used to be, when he was Mr. Man and the only police inside his house was on a TV screen. This new normal of his was shriveling up his spirit into a raisin.

Linzer, the strong, silent type, had simply lowered his head for a moment—a tight, economical motion.

After they left, the house felt strange, no longer homey, like a borrowed and stretched-out jacket or a car loaned and returned with all the settings messed up. The Muffin Man walked around slowly from room to room. They were careful at least. In the TV crime dramas he favored, police searches tended to have a tornado-like effect on a place. Here, things were just slightly out of order. He began straightening out, huffing with indignation.

The kitchen was the worst. Maybe because it was always his least favorite place to clean. There was less to organize now that he lived alone, but still entirely too many things, some of which he wasn't sure he wanted or needed around.

The kitchen always used to be Cherry's domain. He'd cringe at the stereotype of it all had she not been such an amazing cook. Besides, she always seemed to genuinely enjoy it.

Or maybe it was all a lie, the way their wedding vows turned out to be. Till death do us part, my buns, he thought rather contemptuously. What a joke.

It was official—the case was making him sour and bitter. He'd always been a reasonably happy, easy-going guy. The difference was notable and lamentable.

He finished up in the kitchen and went back to the couch to wallow.

The TV wasn't doing the trick of distracting him. All he kept thinking of were the things they took. How little effort would it take to ascribe guilt to the most ordinary household items or internet searches? How easy would it to be view an innocent man through the lens of suspicion and declare his intentions sinister?

The Muffin Man didn't like the way the truth suddenly felt so unsteady, so malleable. He liked numbers and certainty and uncomplicated, predictable things. It may not have made him very exciting or won him many friends or kept his marriage alive, but it was his way, set and comfortable. The sky was blue, the grass was green, and everything in between the two made perfect sense.

But now there were grey clouds above him and red grass on his lawn, strangers in his house, and terrible things looming ahead.

It was enough to upset any man.

He shook the thoughts off bodily, like a dog coming in from the rain. Maybe that's all he needed, some fresh air. He opened one of the back windows and stuck his head out tentatively. A whiff of pot came wafting in, courtesy of Flan DeLeche or maybe even his kid brother—how old was he now, anyway?

Flan used to be a wake-and-bake teen, and somehow the smell managed to drift over all the way to the Man residence every time. They took to knowing his habits and keeping the rear windows shut in the mornings. It seemed easier than confronting the DeLeches over their stoner son. Then Flan got locked up, and the pot smell stopped.

A bank robbery. What a dumb crime in this day and age.

The Muffin Man did some mental math, determining it to have occurred seven years ago. Cherry left a few years after that. He wondered if the cracks in their marriage were starting to show way back when, and he had somehow managed to ignore them.

He'd always been so careful. When it came to relationships, he tended to overproof, giving things too much time to rise before taking the next step. With Cherry he had been the most reckless version of himself, and still it wasn't enough in the end.

He'd been too cautious with the kids, too. Waiting and waiting or, to hear Cherry tell it, giving them too much rope. But they turned out all right, didn't they?

The Muffin Man glanced over at the phone guiltily. He'd never before left it off for longer than a few hours, even if there was no one to call. The kids, he should call the kids. Reassure them that Dad was fine.

He practiced basic conversational lines out loud until he hit the happy, even tone of father-of-the-year, then dialed Poppy's number.

"Hello, Daddy-o," she greeted him. In his mind, the image of a punk-rocker-styled young woman overlaid the picture of an adorable kid with Pippi Longstocking braids and freckles dotting her skin like tiny golden raisins. When she was young, Poppy didn't much look like either of her parents, favoring her beloved Babka, Bran's mom, instead. Now she didn't look like anyone in the family at all.

"Hello, daughter of mine," he replied. "How goes it?"

"I found the most awesome new apartment. I'm actually packing right now. Ber is here helping me. Hang on. Let me put you on speaker." She talked like she'd had way too much caffeine.

"Hi, Pops," Berliner's voice came on. Somehow his son had actually managed to retain his childhood sweetness down to round cheeks that blushed raspberry-red at the slightest provocation. Bran had always hoped the world would be kind to his boy, for his boy was much too jelly-soft for the world.

"Hey, kiddo. How are you?"

"I'm good. I may be a dad soon, if you can believe it."

Bran rolled his eyes, glad for eschewing video calls. "I can believe it."

"We're kind of talking and thinking about it right now Taking our time." Berliner sounded much too young for such thoughts and conversations in his father's opinion for all that was worth.

"Good, good. It's a huge decision," the Muffin Man said, trying to sound supportive and nonjudgmental.

He heard the sound of packing tape unrolled and ripped.

"And what's the new apartment like, Poppy?"

"Dad, are you seriously just going to ignore the elephant in the room like that?" she replied, suddenly stern. "Like, we read the news. Well, I mean, we watch the news."

"They are making it seem worse than it is," he said dismissively, keeping a calm and steady tone. "You know how they say the camera adds ten pounds to everyone's appearance? Well, it's the same with reporting. They exaggerate and make everything seem larger than it is."

"Un-huh," Poppy deadpanned. "So there was no dead body found on your lawn?"

He sighed patiently. "No, there was."

"But you're not a suspect?" Berry said at the same time as Poppy put in, "Did you kill him?"

They all laughed. You had to.

"I'm not a suspect nor am I the guilty party," he assured his kids. "The police are simply doing their due diligence, asking questions, and so on."

"What about that Detective Cotta?" Berry asked. "She looks intense on TV."

"She's just..." Bran looked for a word to describe Cotta. "Italian," he finished lamely.

"I think she's kind of hot," Poppy said over the sound of a heavy box being dragged across the floor.

"You think everyone's kind of hot," Berry observed casually.

It was true, too. And it had resulted in some very random dating choices that used to keep the Muffin Man up at night back when Poppy was still living under his roof. Now that she was old enough to make her own decisions and pay for her own mistakes, he had yet to see any proof of maturity. She liked her partners to be all rock-n-roll, which usually resulted in them either being hardheaded and hardhearted or giving them a tendency to roll away at the nearest dip in the road.

"Point is, I don't want you to worry about me," the Muffin Man told both of them. "Everything's fine. I have been shutting my phone off, so you may not be able to always get through. Just until all the hoopla dies down. But everything is fine."

"Okay, Daddy-o," Poppy singsonged. "If you say so."

"Yeah, Pops, sweet," Berliner put in. "Sorry you have to deal with all this."

"Oh, it's okay. Just one of those monkey wrenches life throws in the works."

"I love that expression," Poppy proclaimed. "It makes me think of literal monkeys with wrenches. Like they are mechanics or something."

"I had the best monkey bread the other day," Ber said. "Those monkeys really know what they're doing."

They laughed and joked around for a while, ending the conversation on a perfectly pleasant note. The Muffin Man was pleased to observe that his children went from perfectly lovable tots to moody teens and exasperating young adults to funny, interesting people he genuinely enjoyed knowing and talking to. Their maturity levels were questionable, perhaps, but Bran had always overdone it in that department and look how far it had gotten him—all the way to being a murder suspect. The kids were all right; they'd rise to the occasion if the heat was on.

He couldn't tell them the truth, of course, about everything that was going on, but honesty was a thing one could only take so far, especially with the family.

The Muffin Man sighed. He'd been sighing so much lately, like he was slowly deflating.

"This too shall pass," he tried telling himself.

Like most pep talks, it proved largely useless.

The Muffin Man turned off his phone and made another round of straightening out, before lowering himself back into his recliner and turning on the TV. He should do some work, he considered idly, but knew he wouldn't be able to concentrate. Besides, work turned his brain on, and he craved the opposite.

The TV, mercifully, managed to do the trick.

ELEVEN

"What do you think?" Sheriff S. Trudel asked the pensive detective. She had been on the phone and computer all day, sometimes simultaneously, doing some sort of deep-dive research, downing cup after cup of espresso and disparaging its quality in both English and Italian. Like many things, it sounded better in Italian.

"Have you heard of the Glüten family, Sherrif?"

Sam dug around his mind for any pertinent information. "It sounds familiar," he ventured tentatively.

Cotta gave him a skeptical look but didn't push it. "The Glütens are a Bavarian clan with more money than Croesus. Notoriously private. They operate behind the scenes and like to keep their fingers in as many pies as possible."

Sam's imagination served up remarkably cartoonish-looking villains. He had to hide a smile.

There was a mumble from the back.

"Yes, Deputy Pastry?"

"Puff, please."

"Absolutely not," Cotta said. "What is your question?"

"Who or what is Croesus?"

Cotta slapped her hands loudly and unleashed a delightful string of Italian in Puff's direction, leaving him more confused than he was going in.

"She says you should have been left in the oven to proof longer," Linzer clarified. "It's an expression."

Cotta narrowed her eyes in appreciation at him. "I didn't know you spoke Italian."

"I don't. Dated an Italian once who used to say that to me."

"Ouch." Detective Cotta laughed. The sound was so startlingly new and unexpected that the room fell completely silent. The laughter cut off abruptly like someone switched the channel. Cotta's face resumed its previous seriousness.

"So, the Glüten family, as it turns out, lost a lot of money in the Soggy Bottom scandal. We don't have the exact figures, but it wasn't pretty, and they are not known to be the forgiving kind."

Sam steepled his fingers on his desk. The gesture looked good on police detectives on TV but didn't feel right to him. He interlaced his fingers instead. Ah, better.

"So, what you're saying," he started slowly, "is that this family has a grudge and can afford to hold it. They wait thirty years and boom, the Muffin Man pops up on their radar again. And they dispatch someone to kill him. This Danish fella."

"Maybe." Cotta crumpled some papers on her desk and made a perfect throw into the trash bin. "I mean, he doesn't seem the type, but maybe that's the main idea. Find someone with his own grudge to bear and give them a push in the right direction."

"So, we need to look for any connections between the Glüten family and Remonce?"

"My people are already on it," she said, "but I'd be surprised if anything turned up. When you have that much money, you learn to cover up your tracks."

"But Remonce is dead," Puff piped in, having bounced back from the reprimand like a particularly resilient batch of dough.

"He is indeed." Cotta's smile was small but sharp enough to draw blood. Humoring people was likely not on her list of favorite things to do. "It is quite likely that Mr. Man did not appreciate having people try to kill him."

"He *had* been on edge lately," Sam pointed out. "All those tourists."

"Precisely." Panna Cotta lifted a pointy finger—a milky white digit that culminated with raspberry-red nail polish. "Maybe he already did not feel safe. Maybe he was already walking around with the knife in his pocket. He hears Remonce in his yard, goes out to confront him, and—"

"Murder," Deputy Pastry finished in a voice hushed with awe.

Sam nodded. No matter how much he didn't see Bran as a murderer, the theory made sense. It was certainly the best they had, and the sooner this case would be put to rest, the happier the sheriff investigating it would be.

"Just have to wait on those tests to come back," he said. They got the knives from the kitchen, the ones that looked to be the right size. The fact that one of them was found under the sink wrapped in an old towel did look rather suspicious. Was its blade stained with rust or something more sinister? Well, that was for the people who got paid for that sort of thing to find out.

"Why would he just leave him there, though?" Deputy Pastry wondered aloud. "Right out front like that."

"That's actually a reasonable question," Cotta said. "What do you think, Deputy Pastry?"

Puff blushed intense red. He didn't do well in the spotlight, looking ready to fall apart under pressure.

Cotta pivoted her attention. "Linzer?"

Deputy Linzer's large head snapped to attention. "Shock," he supplied earnestly. "Mr. Man isn't a seasoned killer. The act had to have left him in shock."

"People just do that?" Puff marveled. "Just walk away like that, leaving bodies in their front yard?"

"I've seen worse," Linzer said gravely, obliquely referring to his military record, occasionally mentioned but never discussed in detail. Sam Trudel saw some paperwork upon hiring Linzer—it was heavily redacted.

"I need some air." Cotta walked outside, her heels punctuating each step in the staccato rhythm reminiscent of her spoken English.

It was a nice day. The air was fresh and crisp, and all Panna wanted was to pollute it with some nicotine. She had quit smoking the year before at her partner's urging and still craved the fix desperately from time to time.

Like many things given up at someone else's insistence rather than on one's own accord, there was a mild resentment associated with quitting. She missed the ritual, the taste of it, the calming sensation that rushed in immediately following the first inhale.

Back home, where smoking was infinitely more popular and less frowned upon than in this weird little place, she used to indulge with a furiousness that had earned her the nickname *drago*—not even the female form of the word, she boasted proudly. Here she would just have to prove herself a dragon in some other way.

The case was turning out to be more interesting than Cotta had originally anticipated. She had always appreciated a good backstory, be it in a book or an investigation. But she wasn't a part of this community, and the outcome didn't much matter to her one way or another. It would, she thought, make a nice notch on the bedpost of her career achievements and hopefully, lead to bigger and better assignments.

Besides, she secretly loved impressing Bistar "Bis" Cotti. The way her partner's tough, grizzled face would light up was always worth it. After the last time she managed to dazzle him, he presented her with a Montblanc's Meisterstück pen.

"Do you know what it means?" he asked, smiling.

She turned the pen over—black, slick, with platinum trim. She knew it couldn't have been cheap and was profoundly moved by the gesture.

"Masterpiece," Cotti told her. "That's what. You and that pen deserve each other now."

It remained one of her most valuable possessions all this time. At the end of the day, she liked to jot down her notes with it. There was a vague idea floating around somewhere in the back of her mind about eventually retiring and writing crime novels. But who knew what the future held? By then, she'd likely be fed up with crime in all shapes and forms. It was draining in a way, to see the worst of humanity, day in and day out. Every commandment disobeyed. Demolished. Her Catholic family would blanche in horror whenever she used to bring work up. She stopped doing that. And then, gradually, she stopped seeing them outside of holidays, citing business instead or a more accurate disinterest.

She never wanted to start one of her own, either. Families seemed like nothing more than a hindrance. None of the great detectives of her beloved mysteries had any. Her job provided camaraderie, companionship, intellectual stimulation. It was plenty.

She cracked her knuckles—one of the twitch-like habits she picked up in the wake of quitting cigarettes —and thought about this place: so quaint, so charming. How impossible it seemed for a murder to find its way here, into this enclave of cozy domesticity. Takes all kinds, she supposed.

Detective Cotta took one more deep breath, trying to enjoy the unadulterated purity of it, and went back inside.

TWELVE

Crazy what a difference seven years made, especially when one person spent them locked up among some of the vilest individuals one might ever have the misfortune to encounter, and the other had enjoyed an easy life in a quiet town.

His partner-in-crime was older, but their age disparity, once so apparent, was barely noticeable now.

Flan still got a hug and a "You look good, man" from the him but he wasn't buying it.

"Got my money?" he asked, skipping the small talk.

"Come on, man, don't be like that. It's been seven years. We need to catch up. Celebrate."

"I'll celebrate when I can afford it," Flan mumbled. "For that, I need my money." He'd never been particularly assertive, and his insistence tended to pale next to his partner's gregarious bonhomie. It made him feel like a dope, like someone who gets talked into things and ends up taking a fall for them. He hated that feeling.

"As I've said before, I'm doing my very best to pull the funds together. I am here, in person, aren't I, to reassure you personally of my most honorable intentions."

It would sound stupid out of anyone else's mouth, but the man made it work. Must have been the way he talked. That ridiculous confidence.

"Okay, well, can you give me something now?" Flan said, hating the pleading notes in his tone. "Just to tie me over."

"Tide."

"What?"

"It's tide me over, that's the expression."

Flan felt the familiar itch of the temper clawing at the back of his mind. The casual correction, the implication of superiority it carried, made him see red. In prison, he'd seen people shivved for less. Rapid fire jabs, rat-tat-tat, and nothing left but a body bleeding out. Flan had always liked knives; any blade, really. Liked the way it made murders personal and intimate, the way they were supposed to be. If you hated someone enough to kill them, you should want to do it up close and personal. Hate was like love in that way, it required proximity.

He imagined the man in front of him bleeding out. Would anyone come help in time? They were meeting out of the way in an abandoned overgrown park the town couldn't decide whether to renovate or tear down. People who came here were not exactly upstanding citizens. The hooded lurking figures that passed by weren't the sort to call the cops.

For as quaint as the town was, this area had a distinctly unsavory flavor.

But would Flan get any of his money if the man was dead? And what if his parole officer were to find out? He did not imagine Officer Struffolli would take to the news kindly. The man was small and round with a voice like honey drip, but there was steel in his eyes and a crack of whip in his tone, too. Flan had seen it and never wanted to be on the receiving end of it.

"Got anything to tide me over?" he repeated, exaggerating the corrected word.

The man eyed him for a moment, then whipped out his wallet and produced a small stack of cash.

Flan took it and riffled through the bills. More dough than he'd seen in a long time, but nowhere near what he was owed.

"When will you have the rest?" he asked, pocketing the money.

"End of the month is my hope," the man replied.

Flan grunted.

"How's things, though? Family treating you okay?"

Flan went to grunt again but diversified by producing a shrug instead.

"Don't worry, once you have the money, you can buy all the love and respect you want," the man said, beaming a bright smile at him. "People are like that, sadly. That's just the way the cookie crumbles."

"You got that?" Flan asked, genuinely curious. "All the love and respect you want? You bought that for yourself, with our money?"

His former partner-in-crime looked at him thoughtfully, then brushed his hands on his immaculate-looking chinos. 'I'd like to think I earned some of it, too, but I try to be realistic."

Flan didn't think it was much of an answer. "Can we meet again next week? Same place, same time? You can give me some more cash while I wait."

"Sure, yeah, okay. As you wish, partner." The way it was said made Flan cringe. He'd never been great at picking out irony, but he wondered if that was it.

They got up to leave, saw a police car drive by, and sat back down immediately, in unison. The vehicle had no sirens on and was out of view soon enough.

The man laughed at their reaction. Flan didn't think it was very funny.

"Think they saw us?" Flan asked, feeling his armpits dampen despite the judicial application of extra-strength vanilla-scented deodorant that morning. Fear always made him sweat.

"You worry too much." There was that smile again. In another world, Flan would like to punch it off. "We're not doing anything wrong, you know. Just two people, socializing."

"Sure. Yeah." Flan got up again. "See you next week?"

"You bet." The man offered his hand, and Flan shook like a trained dog, feeling all kinds of simmering resentment.

They parted ways, and Flan watched his old partner-in-crime saunter away. Such a carefree walk. Such nice clothes. A good haircut, too. Would this be him eventually, once he got his money and left this place? Would someone ever look at him and think "There goes a man without a care in the world?"

One could only hope.

Flan sighed and decided the best way to cheer himself up would be to engage in some retail therapy. He pulled up his hood, and walked back to the town's center, thinking of all the things he could buy. He kept his hands in his pockets, touching the money, making sure it was still there, the entire way.

THIRTEEN

They came for him in the morning. There were those heavy knocks on the door, loud enough to only mean bad news. The Sherrif's face sealed the deal: grim, reluctantly authoritative, almost apologetic.

"You're under arrest," he said. And then there were other words; words the Muffin Man had only ever heard on television, addressed to criminals. It didn't feel real. None of it.

Linzer was there, too. And Cotta.

Trudel had the decency to ask him if he'd like to change, but for the life of him, the Muffin Man couldn't bring himself to care about anything as trivial as clothes. He was led away wearing a pair of old pajamas Cherry got him a long time ago and an only slightly newer brown terry cloth robe. It flapped behind him, making him look like the world's lamest superhero as he was escorted down the driveway and into the back seat of a police car.

There were people outside, though he couldn't tell if it was more of the looky-loos or the media. Either way, photos were being taken. He heard the tell-tale clicks and cringed under all the attention.

The drive was quick, but the town looked different through the back windows of a police vehicle —like a place he hardly knew, not the one he spent his entire life in.

In the station, he was uncuffed and seated in a small plain room across a cheap table from Trudel and Cotta, with Linzer looming in the corner like some kind of deputized monolith.

"Water?" S. Trudel offered. "Coffee?"

The Muffin Man shook his head.

"We would like to give you another chance to tell us about what happened with Niels Remonce," the Italian detective started calmly.

"Who?" His voice sounded creaky with disuse, or maybe stress.

"Niels Remonce," Cotta repeated, her accent giving the name extra syllables. "The Danish man found dead on your lawn."

"I already told you, I don't know him. I don't know anything about what happened."

Cotta pursed her lips. "They say confession is good for the soul."

The Muffin Man eyed her with something like incredulity.

"Before we proceed, are you sure you don't want an attorney present, Mr. Man?" Trudel almost looked sincerely concerned. "Bran?"

He had turned down the offer earlier, thinking, perhaps not clearly, that he had nothing to hide, and a lawyer present might make him seem guilty. He didn't know anyone to call anyway and feared the expense of a private attorney might be way out of his budget. Would a court-appointed one be any good? On TV, they were often too young or too tired, or too underpaid to care or be of much use.

"What's this all about?" Bran asked, hoping to keep the tremble out of his voice.

"We found a knife," Detective Cotta said. "In your kitchen."

"I have a bunch of knives in my kitchen," he responded. "Most people do."

"This one was under the sink, had blood on it, and matched the murder weapon."

He opened his mouth and closed it. There was nothing to say. He felt himself sinking deeper into the murky waters of surrealness he had entered earlier that morning.

Everyone waited patiently, staring at him.

"I didn't kill anyone," he told them.

More silence.

"I wouldn't have kept the murder weapon if I did."

The silence turned heavier, and the Muffin Man figured he should stop talking, quit while he was nowhere near ahead. When was the last time he had cleaned under his kitchen sink? he wondered. No answer came. It simply wasn't a place he kept anything important in or had much use for.

"Did he come after you, Bran?" Sam Trudel said in the warmest, most understanding, man-of-the-people voice he had. "Did he threaten you? Self-defense is a perfectly reasonable reaction, you know."

The Muffin Man sat quietly, chewing his lip. It tasted like raisins, he noticed idly, from the cereal he had for breakfast. The flakes were stale, and there was no fresh milk, so he ended up adding water. A very sad breakfast indeed. Now, who knew when and what he would be eating next?

"Maybe I should get that attorney," he said finally. Then he sat back, crossed his arms, and uttered nothing more until one arrived.

"Terrance Rifle." The handshake was inauspiciously soft. The accent was British. He handed his cards around. "T. Rifle" they read. "As in no one you'd trifle with," he joked clumsily, and straightened out, brushing down his cheap-looking suit.

The TV shows were right. The Muffin Man groaned inwardly. Young, definitely underpaid. T. Rifle did not look tired, though. Quite the opposite, he seemingly buzzed with a very specific brand of overcaffeinated energy.

Bran was left alone with the lawyer to talk things over. Outside of once again professing his innocence, he didn't know what to say.

"Don't worry," T. Rifle said. "The truth will win out. The Sheriff is a fair man. If you are innocent, you have nothing to worry about."

But the Muffin Man did worry. Rifle's presence wasn't particularly reassuring. The room was suffocating. All of this felt like a particularly nasty dream he just couldn't seem to wake up from.

"Just tell the truth," T. Rifle said, scraping with his fingernail at the small stain on his tie—a gaudy thing with fruit designs on it. His fingers were thin and delicate. Lady fingers. "Seriously. It'll set you free." The lawyer smirked, and the Muffin Man felt a quick stab of anger, followed by a slow spread of despair.

The police returned to the room. Everyone re-assumed their positions, except that now T. Rifle was perched to his left on another institutional grey metal chair.

"Interview resuming," Cotta announced for the record. "The client's attorney, T. Rifle, is now also present."

What followed felt to the Muffin Man like a ping-pong match of the most uncomfortable variety.

"Mr. Man, when did you first meet Niels Remonce?"

"I've never met him."

"Does this knife look familiar?"

"Yes, it looks like the one from my kitchen set."

"Looks like it or is it?"

"I can't say. These were not fancy knives, just a mass-produced brand from a box store. My ex-wife and I got them as a wedding gift, I believe."

"Why did you put this one under the sink?"

"I didn't."

"How did it end up under your sink?"

"I have no idea."

"You live alone, correct?"

"Yes."

"Any visitors?"

" Besides you? No. Wait. Yes."

"Which is it?"

"My ex-wife, Cherry, came over the other day."

"Where did you spend time together?"

"In the kitchen. She cooked us a meal."

"Were you together the entire time?"

"I think so. Yes."

"Do you have any reason to believe or any evidence to support a theory that someone might have broken into your house in the last few weeks?"

Silence.

"Shall I repeat the question?"

"No. Not... No evidence."

"Whose fingerprints would you expect to find on your knives if tested?"

"Mine. Maybe my family's. I don't know. I only use one or two of those knives, the rest have just been sitting there, in their wooden block, like swords in the stone, for ages."

"Have you ever committed a violent crime?"

"No."

"Have you ever considered committing a violent crime?"

"No."

"Not once?"

"Not seriously. No."

That earned a raised eyebrow.

"Do you believe in the right to stand your ground and defend your property at all costs?"

"That's a complicated question."

"Yes or no, please."

"In theory, yes."

"Would you protect your property at all costs?"

"I don't know how to answer that. *All costs* seems too vague."

"Would you kill to protect your property?"

Silence.

"Would you kill to pro—?"

"I don't think so."

"Would you kill to protect your life?"

"Maybe. If the circumstances were right. But my life hasn't been in danger, and I did not kill anyone. To protect it or otherwise."

"Would you say the last month has been particularly stressful? Ever since the rhyme came out? Ever since your address became public knowledge?"

"Yes."

"Would you say the stress was negatively impacting your life?"

"It was upsetting."

"Enough to make a complaint to the Sheriff?"

"I just wanted them to leave me alone."

"You missed your privacy?"

"Yes. Yes, I did."

"Do you value your privacy?"

"Yes, very much."

"Enough to defend it?"

"Within reason. Yes."

"Enough to kill for it?"

"No. Emphatically no."

Silence.

The Muffin Man glared at his attorney, who sat there seemingly amused by the back and forth. "You don't want to chime in?" he asked the man with barely masked irritation.

"Oh no, you're doing great," T. Rifle said. "Really."

He could see that Detective Cotta was enjoying this. Her normally pale complexion had acquired something like a blush. Sam Trudel, on the other hand, looked like he wanted to be anywhere but here. Linzer remained his usual unreadable self.

The questions began again. The same things worded slightly differently as if trying to catch him out on a lie. Bran had seen that trick on TV, and thought he managed to dodge the pratfalls nicely.

When they took another break, he felt a bit out of breath, like he had just run a short but grueling marathon. He asked for water and downed an entire glass of it, trying not to think about whether it made him look guilty or not.

"So, let me get this straight," said Trifle when the police came back, ready to proceed with their inquiries. He had finally finished fidgeting with his tie and seemed suddenly and sharply focused. "Everything you have is purely circumstantial. You have no witnesses, no proof, nothing. Your best hope is to get my client's confession, which he has declined to do, insisting on his innocence."

"Strong circumstantial evidence," Linzer put in, his voice low and heavy.

"There have been people near my client's property for weeks. The house has no alarm system, right?"

Bran realized the question was addressed to him and nodded.

"No security cameras?"

Bran nodded again.

"Okay, so no alarms, no security," Trifle went on, gaining momentum. "Anyone with the most rudimentary physical ability could have entered the premises, taken and replaced the knife. You have not established any connection between my client and the victim. You have not established a motive."

If looks could kill, Detective Cotta's expression would have done to T. Rifle what a bakery slicer does to a fresh loaf.

"Despite my accent, I am very well-versed in the local law," the attorney went on. "I think we all know the case you have against my client is thinner than a crème brûlée's crust. So why don't we arrange for something mutually agreeable? Unless you'd rather risk a charge of violating my client's civil liberties?"

The Jekyll and Hyde transformation of Terrance Rifle was so striking, it effectively whiplashed people in the room into a stunned silence. When the conversation resumed, the tone was different.

The rest was motions. The Muffin Man submitted himself to the process, letting it carry him the way the waves in the ocean might a boat. He no longer assumed any agency in this life. How arrogant he'd once been to think he ever had any. Other people were in charge. Events occurred of no volition of his own.

If he were a boat, he'd let T. Rifle chart the course, since the man had proven himself to be eminently skilled with the oars.

The Muffin Man got lost in the metaphor. Or was it a simile? He was tired. All he wanted to do was go home. If he dug any deeper into that desire, he might discover a wish to disappear altogether. From a muffin to a crumb to nothingness.

Terrance Rifle snapped him out of the maudlin thoughts.

"You're being released. For now. Ankle monitor and best behavior, okay?" He winked. "Don't worry," he repeated his mantra like repetition could make it come true. "Nothing to worry about. The truth will find a way."

The Muffin Man sighed heavily and allowed himself to be fitted with a plastic device. It looked too simple to be high-tech, but what he knew of modern technology was lamentably little.

"This one is GPS-based," Linzer explained. "It'll know your exact position. You can stay in your house, you can go to the yard. Anything further will trip it."

"That's an unusually restrictive length," Rifle argued. "Perhaps we could..."

"No, it's okay," the Muffin Man interrupted. "It's okay, really. I have no plans to go anywhere."

It sounded better that way than admitting to having nowhere to go.

He was driven back home in the Sheriff's car. No sirens. They took the backroads to Drury Lane, presumably to avoid the press. He stared out of the window the entire time. The place still did not look exactly familiar, but perhaps it was because he was being driven past an area he never went to--an abandoned park on the town's outskirts that everyone knew was generally frequented by various delinquents and people up to no good. Therefore, the Muffin Man wasn't particularly surprised to see Flan DeLeche hanging out there. But the man Flan was with surprised him greatly. He even did a double take, turning in his seat as far as he could for another look. It was definitely him. But why?

FOURTEEN

Detective Panna Cotta did not like the lawyer with the British accent. She didn't care for how deceptively incompetent he seemed at first, and how swiftly he changed his tune when the push came to shove. In her experience, most defense attorneys were scum, either by nature or by association. Nevertheless, Terrance Rifle had a point. They needed something more solid. The binding agent that would unite all the disparate ingredients of the case into one coherent dough of a case. A confession would have been ideal, but the Muffin Man was either legitimately innocent or a world-class actor.

Secretly, she hoped it was the latter, because the former implied starting over from scratch, and she was so very ready to be done with this case and this—what was the word?—Podunk town.

Cotta phoned Bis, who reminded her of the virtue of patience. She told him she'd like to see how virtuous he'd be if he had to drink the swill that passed for espresso here day in, day out. He laughed. She laughed. For a moment, she felt better.

"What if he *is* innocent?" Cotti posited. "What if it's something else you're not even considering? Don't get blinkered by the obvious." It was just the sort of thing he liked to say. Over the years, Panna had taken it in as one of her own personal credos, a page in the rulebook to live by. "Remember the Beignets?"

"Of course." How could she forget the Beignets? The Beignet crime family practically ran Paris for a full decade before being undone by their rivalry with the Palmiers. All over a dessert recipe, of all things, the pride and joy of the families' respective matriarchs. The Beignet twins—Maman Choux's favorite little nightmares, not to mention her most efficient henchmen—destroyed by a rivalry that had nothing to do with crime. Until, of course, it did. Baking, it seemed, could be dangerous when done right. Lethal, even.

The streets of Paris ran red for weeks because two old women could not agree on which one of them held the secret to the most perfectly flaky crust. Imagine that.

The case had become a textbook study of subverted expectations. Criminals, everyone was reminded, were more than... well, criminals. They were people with ideas and families and thoughts and feelings, a lot of which often had nothing to do with their lawbreaking. People as complicated, fallible, and absurd as the rest. There were a million reasons to commit a crime, any crime, especially murder.

So then, who wanted to kill a random middle-aged Danish tourist on a lawn of a random semi-retired middle-aged local man and why? What was she not seeing?

That night Cotta could not sleep. She spent a few hours researching everyone connected to the case, using both local and international databases, then lay in bed staring at the streetlight-streaked ceiling and turning the facts over in her head, making them fit. It was like a jigsaw puzzle. Until the pieces were locked together, she could not see the grand picture.

As much as she wanted to go home, she didn't wish to be responsible for putting the wrong man in jail. Or, worse yet, letting the real killer get away.

Her parents were killed by a random assailant who was never caught. Someone she was once in a relationship with referred to it as her Batman origin story. The relationship ended shortly after. The hunger for justice remained. It fueled her waking hours and kept her up at night.

Just as her eyelids began to feel heavy, and sleep finally came knocking down her door, Cotta had an inkling of an idea. Just a flicker, really. But it was worth looking into. She thought about reaching for her phone to leave herself a note but fell asleep before she could.

She dreamed of the Beignet twins. In life, no one could ever tell them apart, but in death, their expressions were starkly different, like masks of comedy and tragedy. And then Cotti came and took the gun out of her hands, and the dream ended.

FIFTEEN

Days passed with barely anything to distinguish them from one another. He watched too much TV and wallowed. He didn't eat enough. From time to time, Terrance came over and brought food and updates.

First impressions be damned, T. Rifle turned out to be a genuinely nice guy, not to mention a surprisingly effective lawyer. The legalese made the Muffin Man feel tired and out of his depth, but he understood the gist of things: though they could not prove his guilt, there was simply too much evidence, circumstantial or otherwise, to dismiss the case against him outright.

And all the while, there was one nagging thought circling the drain of his mental sink. During the day, he tried to busy himself to deny its existence, but at night, it roared at him, larger in the dark like all monsters.

It wasn't merely a case of avoiding the truth—he simply didn't know what to do with it. If what he thought was even the truth. It began with a kernel of an idea and over time morphed into a distinct possibility, but he was yet to understand the "whys" of it.

The Muffin Man prided himself on being a reasonable man.   Not understanding the reason behind something was driving him mad. He turned it over and over in his mind, like a puzzle box, looking for a way in. And then there was that pesky fear of figuring it out, too. What would it mean for him? For his world at large? Some truths could do that—upend all you knew.

It was no good to be a reasonable man in an unreasonable world. He always thought he belonged here, that this place had a mold with his shape, and he fit into it precisely. It was a comforting, warm feeling. Now it was gone.

There was nothing T. Rifle could say or do to change it. Though, to his credit, he did try.

He brought the Muffin Man's mail in, including the newspapers. The Muffin Man had managed to avoid those until now, but he didn't have it in him to rebuke a gesture meant in kindness.

He didn't mean to look, but the headlines were right there, screaming at him: "Do You Know The Muffin Man?" It was all variations on the same theme. That same stupid rhyme. Apparently, after being a part of the community for all of his life, he was suddenly an unknown, potentially dangerous, quantity. A persona non... something.

Bran pushed the papers aside, but the damage was done, the kind of subtle erosion of a person's spirit that could be difficult to quantify and nearly impossible to come back from.

The headlines were gimmicky. The newspapers were likely selling out like hotcakes.

"What if I had an idea, a theory really, about the killer?" he asked his attorney.

Terrance brightened up, pushing his tea aside. "Oh, do tell."

"No, no, it isn't... I mean, I'm not sure. I just... would you have to tell Trudel and Cotta?"

"Anything you share with me is private," the attorney assured him. "But I may do some sleuthing on my own based on your theory, see if we can find the killer, since the police seems to be moving molasses-slow on this."

The Muffin Man clocked the wording—it was nice to be believed in. At least someone didn't think he was a murderer.

Rubbing the back of his neck, he voiced his uncertainty. "I'm worried about being wrong. Don't want to stir anything up. I wish I could do the sleuthing myself."

Terrance folded his mouth into something like casual sympathy, the way adults do when they have to tell the kids that something is off-limits.

"I know, I know," Bran said with a sigh. "Can't have my cake and eat it too, right?"

"Something like that."

Or maybe it was nothing like that. The metaphor seemed apt when first spoken but came undone upon closer examination.

"I'm sure it will be solved, eventually," Terrance offered kindly, taking the pressure off his client. "The police..."

"Yeah, I don't have much trust in powers that be these days," Bran said, finishing his tea. Now that his only visitor was English, he drank an awful lot of tea.

"Don't sneak out and do anything you'll end up regretting," T. Rifle told him later, on his way out. "This house arrest thing is a win. Do not jeopardize it."

The Muffin Man reassured him that he wouldn't. What was one more lie now that he was seemingly caught in a web of them?

After the attorney left, Bran put on his headphones and listened to some music.

The usual suspects weren't cutting it. Sugarloaf failed to weave its psychedelic charm on him. Martha and the Muffins didn't take him to Echo Beach. He shut the music off and let the rushing of the static hit his ears like ocean waves. Far from calming, it pulled and pushed him. *Do something, say something*, it seemed to urge.

He shook his head. "And if I'm wrong?"

And if you're right? the audio waves countered.

All his life things had more or less made sense. The Muffin Man had never felt like he was at the mercy of some mysterious dark powers pulling his strings. He'd been happy or sad, he'd won or lost, but he was never helpless. Until now.

He tried the phone but hung up before the call connected. It was the sort of thing to discuss face-to-face. You had to see the eyes of the person. And it still might not be enough.

In that one respect, the newspapers had it right—you never really knew anyone.

The Muffin Man imagined sneaking outside, daring to trip the signal with the device on his ankle, going and confronting...

But in the end, he didn't have to. In the end, the person came to him. He didn't even have to wait all that long.

At first, he thought it was Terrance returning, and surprised by how soon it was since the last visit, went to answer the door.

It wasn't Terrance.

"Hi," the Muffin Man offered a simple greeting and stepped back, letting his visitor through. "I've been expecting you," he said, once the door closed behind them; his words a combination of the truth, trepidation, and wishful thinking.

They stared at each other for a while with something like weary resignation.

"I know," said one pair of eyes.

"I'm sorry," replied the other.

"Tea?" he asked out of habit.

'Sure."

The Muffin Man sighed—he seemed to sigh so much these days like simple breathing no longer did the trick—and put the kettle on.

SIXTEEN

"I think we need to look closer at Flan DeLeche," Cotta said, on her second cup of espresso and hating it.

"Didn't we, though?" S. Trudel shifted uncomfortably in his chair. "I mean, his parole officer says he's been staying out of trouble, and I don't want to ruffle the DeLeches' feathers any more than we have to."

"Hear me out." Cotta pushed her cup away, neatly avoiding splashing her latest creamy-white outfit. "This is a low-crime town by any standard, right?"

"Yep." Trudel nodded. "And proud of it."

"You've got what? One known criminal here?"

This was technically true. Ginger was serving a life sentence elsewhere. Trudel gave another nod.

"But not really, though, right?" Cotta pushed on.

Sam furrowed his brow.

"I've gone over Flan's case. He had an accomplice. One you never caught." Sam shifted again. Cotta noticed his discomfort as she went on. "One Flan never gave up. What if he was local, too? I mean, it makes sense. Flan wasn't a well-traveled young person. Records show he never left the country. Only left this town a few times, as a kid. So, say his partner-in-crime was someone he met locally. And say, for some reason, this person stayed local. Which seems likely because this town, it's that kind of place, isn't it? I hear of people moving here but never moving away. Like Hotel California. You can never leave."

Deputy Paul "Puff" Pastry walked in on the last line and immediately started humming the song. Cotta arched her eyebrows at him like tightly-strung bows until he stopped.

"So then," she continued, turning her attention back to Sam, "this person, the other bank robber, likely the mastermind, gets the money, right? Because they never found any on Flan. Presumably, they worked out some sort of a deal at the time. And then you have someone with a lot of dough, and no one to come looking for it for a long time."

"So, he stayed in town is what you're saying?" the Sheriff summed up.

"Let's assume that he did, having no real reason to leave."

"Flan *would* be getting out eventually, though," Trudel pointed out. "His partner knew that."

"But the key word is *eventually*." Cotta produced something like a grin. "I don't think this person thought very far ahead. I don't think we're dealing with the smartest of criminals here. Besides, they might have had other reasons to stay."

"Uh-huh." Sam nodded. "Right."

"So I started looking at anyone in town demonstrating conspicuous wealth around the time of Flan's sentencing."

"And?"

"And nothing. Apparently, they were smart enough to wait. So then me and Linzer started moving the timeline until we found someone to fit the bill."

"Really?" Sam slid closer to the edge of his seat. "Who?"

Cotta smiled triumphantly, looking like a shark who had just spotted a particularly juicy-looking surfer, and pushed a file across the desk toward Trudel. He opened it and studied the photo. "Well, I'll be..." he said eventually.

"We did some more checking, too. It's all in there. An unsavory past buried beneath a freshly-baked façade."

S. Trudel read the papers in front of him, his frown deepening with each paragraph.

"Right under our noses." He harrumphed. "Why not just leave?"

"That's the thing, according to this—" Detective Cotta stabbed a long finger at one of the pages of the financial records; red nail polish sharply contrasting the white paper. "—there was a tentative plan to leave but not right away. Remember, Flan wasn't due out. His getting paroled early was a surprise. And here, it looks like the plans to leave got pushed forward recently. Aggressively so. There's the real estate listing. Private, you'll notice."

Sam shook his head as if to physically clear his mind. "Okay, okay," he said, louder than intended. "But what does any of it have to do with Remonce?"

"Well. "Cotta pressed her lips into a thin bloodless line for a moment before releasing them audibly. "That's the thing I'm not sure about. But I think, maybe... nothing?"

"Come again?"

"Wrong time, wrong place as you say. Just being across the way from a volatile young man fresh out of prison and harboring a temper problem?"

"Flan? Really?" Sam rubbed his chin. "He seems like such a mild young man. Troubled, sure, but not violent. He was caramel-sweet as a kid."

Cotta pushed another file at Sam. "His prison records say otherwise. He almost got killed once apparently but managed to fight his attacker off."

Sam couldn't help but feel a bit impressed. "They still let him out early though, with all this?"

Cotta flicked her fingers at him in a gesture that was either meant to represent fireworks or exasperation. "Overcrowding."

"Right, right." Trudel looked at the papers before him, disliking this feeling of being shown up, but appreciating the proximity of a satisfactory solution.

"So, shall we go have a chat with...?"

Linzer's phone began going off. "Sorry." He grabbed it. "It's my alarm."

Deputy Pastry smirked. "Was that...?"

"Yes, Paul, it was "Birthday Cake" by Rihanna. I like Rihanna, okay?"

"Sure, sure." Puff backed away, still smirking.

"Apologies for the interruption," Linzer announced, "but looks like the Muffin Man is out of bounds."

"Well, I guess we know where we're going first." Sam got up with a grunt.

"How difficult is it to stay inside your house?" Cotta groaned. "I swear, the criminal element in this town is so..."

"Half-baked?" Puff offered helpfully.

"I was going to say soft, Deputy Pastry, thank you."

They drove fast, and this time they used a siren.

SEVENTEEN

"So," the Muffin Man began slowly, "Baguette..."

"He doesn't know I'm here," Cherry said, toying with her teacup.

"But does he know about...?"

She looked at him with the same beautiful eyes he fell in love with decades ago, and for an instant, their world was suspended in a Schrödinger-style uncertainty.

And then she blinked, and it was all over.

"Why, Cherry?"

"Because..." She exhaled softly, letting the sentence hang unfinished. They used to talk for hours on end, never wanting to stop. Over time, their conversation ebbed into mostly comfortable silences. Then less comfortable. Then there was nothing but silences punctuated with cautiously polite exchanges.

And now, they've come to a place of letting ellipses do the talking for them.

Bran waited patiently until she began to speak in earnest.

"I'm tired. I used to brush off my mistakes but now they linger. They eat at me. I've made a mistake with us, I know that now. Another one with French. And more and more..."

"I saw him with Flan the other day," he told her softly. "It's what got me thinking about things."

"We never talked about it." She shook her head to emphasize the point. "I think I just didn't want to know. It was all brand-new and exciting and fun."

"Was it the money?" Bran asked. "I've always wondered. That house of his, the fancy car. And I never really made that much."

"I wish it was as simple as the money." Cherry sighed. There were tears in her eyes now, clinging to mascaraed eyelashes precariously, poised to drop at any moment. "He... he made me feel young."

"You are," the Muffin Man said.

"No, I'm not." She sighed again, sadder. "Not anymore. It's like something shifted once I hit fifty, and I could see—I could *feel*—every wrinkle, every age spot, every grey hair. And French, he's into older women. He made me forget."

Bran hoped he kept his cringing inwardly. There were certain things a man shouldn't have to hear about the love of his life.

"So, what went wrong?" he asked after a while.

"Flan got out. That was the beginning of the end." Cherry shook her head, and a stray tear departed her eyelashes to roll down her cheek. "No, that's a lie. It all started before that. The problem with newness is that you can't sustain it. Every fresh thing gets stale. You just gotta learn to love the flavor enough to tolerate the staleness, and French and I didn't have that."

We did, Bran thought, but did not say.

"But with Flan out, French had to give him his share of the money."

"Only he didn't have that," Bran supplied. That was the part he figured out first.

"He did not."

"What happened to it? There was so much."

Cherry shrugged. "Lavish spending. Bad investments. You name it. He may have masterminded a bank robbery, but he's no good with money."

Bran nodded understandingly.

"He even asked *me* for money. Imagine the audacity." Cherry wiped her eyes delicately. "Of course, I didn't have any to help him. Wouldn't have even if I did. But it got me thinking that my sweet free ride on that particular showboat was coming to an end. And here I was, middle-aged, useless, and about to become homeless."

Bran nodded again. He knew what was coming, or thought he did, but wanted to hear her say it.

"I was online a lot at that time, just browsing around, de-stressing, trying out different forums<" Cherry went on. "That's where I met Niels. He was so nice, so sweet. Not wanting to repeat the same mistake I've made with French, I researched him and found out about his mother's family and their money. I thought, okay, this time around, I'd be really set."

The Muffin Man smiled sadly. "You didn't dig deep enough."

"I did not." She laughed, but there was no humor in it. "The money was gone. But Remonce remained very much present. I tried to drop him, tactfully at first, then less so, but he just would not take the hint. Said he'd fallen in love with me. And then..."

"He showed up here."

"He showed up here. Professing his love. Making everything worse. Told me he'd stick around until I change my mind. And I was in a bad place at the time mentally. I couldn't sleep. I kept taking these long walks. I'd walk back to Drury, like taking a stroll down memory lane. All I kept thinking about was our lovely house—how careless I was to leave it, and how I'd never be welcome there again.

"French was making me paranoid, so I've taken to carrying a knife in my purse. One of the old kitchen ones from our wedding set. I don't know how I ended up packing it with me when I left. And one very late night or very early morning, depending on how you think of it, I saw Remonce. He was out walking too.

Couldn't sleep due to a vicious jet lag. He said he liked the houses of Drury Lane. I told him I used to live in one. He wanted to see which one. I showed him."

She chewed her red-tinted lip for a moment before continuing. "And then our conversation turned from civil into something much darker. He was such a strange man—he'd go from sweet as honey to nutty as a fruitcake with almost nothing in between. We got into it. Really got into it. I felt threatened. I was sure I acted in self-defense, though looking back on it, the picture is all blurry."

Cherry wiped at her mascara-streaked cheeks and took a sip of her now-tepid tea. Bran just looked at her, a million thoughts running through his head.

"And then you figured why not frame me for the murder?" he said finally.

She hung her head in shame. "I wasn't thinking clearly. You have to believe me. I just thought that maybe that way I'd get the house."

Bran felt his benevolence leak out of him like air out of a punctured tire.

"You came here deliberately," he pointed out. "You planted the knife under my sink. That seems like very clear thinking to me."

She looked up at him with tears in her eyes. The Muffin Man could never stand to see Cherry cry. Even now, he felt his resolve wobble as if experiencing a gravitational shift.

"I was stupid, and I was desperate," she said, emotions choking her voice. "You have no idea what it's like to be a middle-aged woman. A nobody."

"You're not a nobody," he told her gently, the way you'd speak to someone you once—and still—loved. "You're Cherry Tart. And you are a murderer."

Something shifted in her face, a subtle change, but Bran had decades of experience recognizing and reading them.

"You'll tell them?" She met his eyes, searching them, trying to read his mind.

"I won't have to. They'll figure it out. I did."

Cherry cracked her knuckles and spoke very fast. He knew that mode of hers too. She was trying to be persuasive. "You can tell them it was in self-defense. That Remonce confronted you over his family's lost fortune. They'll believe you. People stand their ground all the time. I won't say anything, to anyone. I won't ask you for anything. Ever. Not the house. Not a penny. I'll just... disappear."

The Muffin Man looked at his ex-wife—the familiar face juxtaposed with that of a stranger. How well did we know our loved ones? He imagined a newspaper headline crying "Do You Know Cherry Tart?"

Then he shook his head. "It's too late for all that, Cherry."

She blinked. Another tectonic shift if you knew to look for it.

From some hidden depth of her purse, she produced a knife and pressed it against her neck. "I'll tell them you tried to kill me. That you've been trying to win me back, and my refusal drove you mad."

There was only the ticking of the wall clock to remind them that this was reality and not some strange dream. The Muffin Man said nothing, continuing to shake his head softly. He could see how white her knuckles were. The knife trembled in her hand, grazing the blueish vein on the side of her neck. She applied a bit more pressure. The tender flesh yielded to the blade.

Bran narrowed his eyes. Was it another knife from the same set? How many did she grab when she left? How had he not noticed they were missing? He really should take greater care to pay attention to the finer details of his life.

A knock on the door cut through the tension of the moment. Was it Terrance? The police? Someone from the media sneaking past the sheriff's deputy on duty?

They looked at each other for a moment, startled.

"I have to get that," he said. "It could be the Sheriff."

She paled visibly, with only her cheeks remaining bright red. She did not lower the knife.

Slowly, Bran got up and walked toward the front door. Another surprise guest. What a day. He would have told his visitor off under normal circumstances, however, this was anything but.

Baguette strolled in, looking more harassed than his usual calm and collected self. His hair was in disarray. His shirt looked expensive but wrinkled.

"She is here, no?" he said by way of greeting, looking around wildly. "Cherry? Cherry?" His accent appeared almost exaggerated. Perhaps it was the stress.

Bran waited for the inevitable. The two of them found each other in the kitchen. A screaming match ensued, with Baguette slipping in and out of his native tongue.

The Muffin Man, feeling suddenly like a stranger in his own house, leaned against the wall as casually as a mere observer.

How strange life was, he mused. Full of huge meaningless things and small devastating ones. False leads, false hopes, false proofs. And none of this had anything to do with the Soggy Bottom business after all. What were the odds?

"Oh, shut up," Cherry screamed at her lover, storming out of the kitchen. "You're from Ottawa."

"Gatineau. That's Quebec."

"Who cares?"

They still have the energy and zeal to fight, which was nice, but this wasn't a fight either of them would win.

"I love you, Cherry. Je t'aime. But we have to leave, yes?"

She stopped and stared at him hard. "And where are we going to go, darling?"

"Anywhere but here. I think Flan is going to get violent. I am very concerned. I think maybe he killed that man. That Danish man. And you should not be here. Why are you here? Are you thinking of going back to *him*, Cherry?" The hand gesture in Bran's direction was definitely over the top.

The Muffin Man thought if he saw such theatrics on TV he'd probably laugh. In real life, the tragedy balanced out the comedy into a spectacular-to-behold chaos.

His ex-wife opened the door to step outside. Her lover followed. They made it to the front yard, still a crime scene, screaming at each other. The Muffin Man had never seen Cherry like that and didn't know if it was a good or a bad thing. The passion they inspired in each other once upon a time was always a calm, steady flame. This was a roaring inferno. Someone was bound to get burned.

Baguette reached for Cherry, and she slashed at him with the knife she was still holding. The blade sliced through the skin as easily as it would through warm butter. Baguette screamed and clasped his injured hand.

Staring at them through the doorway, the Muffin Man observed more blood being added to the grass of his front lawn. Something had to be done, and being a lifelong pacifist, he could only think of one thing. He left the house and kept on walking, right past the fighting couple, right past the front gate. Once his slippered feet hit the street's pavement, he continued down Drury Lane very slowly until he heard the cry of approaching sirens. Then he stopped and waited.

EIGHTEEN

F lan heard every word through his bedroom window. The fight on Drury Lane was as unlikely as a snowstorm in Hawaii. And this one was vicious enough to remind him of prison. He recognized the voice of his partner-in-crime, of course—Baguette's accent was pretty inimitable—but it took a moment to process what he was saying.

Leaving, he was leaving, after all this. The money was gone, and he feared for his life. Well, good, Flan thought, feeling oddly proud. He *should* fear. Let him tremble in his designer boots.

But then... the money was gone. The sadness hit Flan potently, flattening him like a rolling pin. All his plans, all his hopes, all his dreams. He knew the possibility of this existed, but he had steadfastly refused to believe it. And now it was here, staring him in the face. Unignorable. Ugly. Real.

The sadness morphed into rage. The shift was sudden, brutal in its swiftness. The rage didn't slowly bubble up to the surface, it was just there. Flan saw red.

He did not see himself leave the house, cross the street, or put his hands on his once friend and partner. And he did not stop sinking his fists into the man's flesh until it felt like nothing more than raw dough. He heard screaming but couldn't tell if it was him or someone else. It didn't matter. The red curtain that had fallen over his eyes let in no light.

NINETEEN

Sheriff S. Trudel could see they were too late before he even left his car. Before they dragged Flan DeLeche off French Baguette's body, handcuffing one and searching for the pulse on the other. Before they pried the knife from Cherry Tart's white-knuckled grasp.

By the time they were done with all that, the Muffin Man's breaking of this ankle monitor's radius seemed like nothing, the most minute of transgressions. After all, he wasn't trying to flee, he was merely summoning help the best way he could at the moment. It worked, too. But still... Trudel shook his head. What a mess.

Sam thought he was done with all that nonsense, figuring that cases like these in a town like theirs came about once in a lifetime. And his lifetime had already had Ginger. But no, here it was again. A freshly-baked nightmare straight out of some Hell-forged oven.

There'd be no re-election now, he mused idly, eyeing the disapproval in the eyes of the neighbors pouring out of their homes onto Drury Lane. It seemed that life had decided to help him make up his mind about early retirement, conveniently and finally.

"What happened?" he asked, not sure whom he was addressing.

"It was Flan and Baguette," the Muffin Man said, rather calmly, considering. "They were behind the bank robbery all those years ago, and their reunion did not go to plan. Cherry came over because she felt threatened. Baguette came after her. Flan came after him. And this happened." He gestured toward his front yard, twice a crime scene now.

"And Remonce?" the obvious question came.

"Remonce was someone Cherry met online. Baguette killed him in a jealous rage."

"On your front lawn?" Cotta asked, suspiciously. "On the anniversary of the Soggy Bottom thing?"

The Muffin Man shrugged. "He was trying to set me up. It seems he was also afraid of Cherry going back to me. A very troubled man, very insecure."

Cotta nodded, thoughtfully, the suspicion never leaving her face.

The Muffin Man didn't care. From what he knew of people, which he had to admit as of late wasn't much, he figured his story might just work. He watched Cherry's face the entire time, the way she composed herself, going from a distraught, devasted woman on the edge to her reporter-special calm, while keeping just enough trauma visible in her expression.

"Can you confirm this, ma'am?"

"Yes," she said, her voice perfectly trembly with tears. "Oh, yes."

It was good enough for Sam Trudel. Another nightmare put to rest, a messy case with a neat resolution. Perhaps if he took the time to really poke and prod the details, he could have massaged out some inconsistencies, but he found he simply didn't have the heart to. After the crime scene was processed, and the statements were taken, and the i's were dotted, and the t's were crossed, he wanted nothing more than to fall asleep in Ruggie's arms. This was it, he knew, he was done. It felt strangely liberating, like a huge weight he didn't know he was carrying was suddenly lifted off his shoulders. Linzer would do a fine job as his successor, he mused. He'd hand down the reigns at the nearest appropriate opportunity. And then, there'd be an easy-as-pie life as far as the eye could see.

Detective Cotta's spidey senses were tingling. The case had the consistency of Swiss cheese. She could stay here and explore it, or she could wrap it up and go home. The details could be rearranged to suit their purpose. One way or another, she did some good here. The crime was solved, after a fashion. And if she knew more about it, she didn't feel the need to enlighten Trudel. In fact, she thought it was all rather romantic.

She smiled a rare genuine smile, something she only did in private and a privileged few had ever witnessed. This case would stay with her, she knew. It got under her skin, though she tried not to let it. She'd think about all this misspent passion late at night, wondering if it was worth it. And in the end, she'd tell herself her solitary ways were better and fall asleep believing it.

It was all lies, really. The stories we told ourselves and others. Some elaborate and some half-baked, some to ruin and some to save.

One day, she thought, this might be a story too. One day she might even write it.

She tried to imagine that future in the evening, before falling asleep, but some days it seemed farther away than others. So, she got out her Meisterstück pen and jotted down a few details and observations just in case.

Then she phoned Bis. He picked up on the second ring.

"Can't sleep?" he asked, eschewing customary greetings.

"No, but we solved the case."

"Oh yeah?" She heard the glog-glog-glog of something being poured into a glass. "Congrats, then. Here's to you."

"Cin-cin," she said, toasting the victory, such as it was, with an imaginary drink.

"When are you coming back?"

"As soon as I get the go-ahead from the main office. Honestly, I can't wait to leave. There's something strange about this place."

"Like what?"

"Like it seems so happy on the surface and beneath it is—" Cotta searched for the word. "—quicksand. It doesn't want to let you go. Everyone seems to just stick around."

"Is it such a bad thing?"

She pressed the phone receiver to her forehead, pondering the question. "I don't know," she said eventually. "I guess I want a bigger sky."

"Piece of cake." Her partner laughed, the same familiar, warm sound. "Come home. We got all the sky in the world."

"I will," she promised. "As soon as I can."

TWENTY

The Muffin Man double-checked his bags. He had packed them methodically, using a list and checking things off one by one, but there was a lot to consider.

The house sold quickly. He made no stipulations as far as potential buyers went. If a looky-loo wanted to snap it up, let them. If some morbid true crime devotee desired it, sell it. The highest bid won. It gave him enough money for what he had in mind.

He had seen Cherry only once since everything. She was moving in with Poppy, temporarily. Bran could just about imagine his ex-wife cringing at the idea of being forced to involuntarily relive her youth in a way, but needs must and all that. She inherited a few things from Baguette, but most had to be sold to cover his extravagant debts.

She talked about this or that as a potential late-in-life career, but to Bran it all sounded like so much pie in the sky. Still, he wished her the best. Sincerely.

They were awkward around each other. Seeing another person's true face could either bring people closer or push them farther apart. And it did not bring them closer.

They were now a kind of intimate strangers. They knew too much of one another for love, though some genuine affection remained. He'd like to believe so.

"I owe you my life," she whispered, hugging him before leaving.

"Well, then," he told her softly, "use it wisely."

Her scent, still delicious, lingered long after she walked away. He watched her leave, feeling perfectly at peace.

No one would watch him leave. Just as he wanted. He'd start in Spain, he had always wanted to visit it. Then go on to Italy, France, Greece. Anywhere the wind blows. He could always work remotely once the funds from the house sale got low. Numbers, after all, could be crunched anywhere.

The Muffin Man intended to see the world. And let the world see him, too. Because, after all, he realized, it did not know him at all. Not really. And it was time to let himself be known.

ACKNOWLEDGEMENTS

All stories start out as simply ideas and words. Once they get turned into books, readership is what makes them come alive. So let me thank the people who helped me and my book on its journey.

Nate Ragolia, Spaceboy Books' wonderful publisher and an even better human being, for seeing this book's potential and for bringing it to life.
Davida De La Harpe Golden for friendship, edits, and believing in me.

Andrew Hook, Lindz McLeod, Ben Jones, William Brandon, and Seb Doubinsky for their kind words and wonderful blurbs.

Papa Sanz for helping to get that cover bloodstain just right.

Atticus Morton, the best superfan an author could ask for.

Michael Marshall Smith, for so many things, including but not limited to being a fantastic interpreter of worlds, real and fictional.

All my fans and supporters for making my writing pursuits seem a somewhat reasonable and almost not at all preposterous / mad / out-there idea.

And last but not least, my endless gratitude to my beautiful wife, Chelsea. I only do this to impress you, and yes, I love you more than muffins.

Oodles of freshly baked gratitude to everyone who bought and read this book. By doing so, you are literally making my dreams come true. Go you, dream maker!

Kindly consider leaving a review on a platform of your choice for that cherry on top.

Until next time!

ABOUT THE AUTHOR

Mia Dalia is an internationally published, CWA-nominated author of all things fantastic, thrilling, scary, strange ... and, occasionally, hilarious.

Her short fiction has been published online by *Night Terror Novels*, *50-word stories*, *Flash Fiction Magazine*, *Pyre Magazine*, *Tales from the Moonlit Path*, *carte blanche magazine*, Jaded Ibis Press, *Weird Wide Web*; in print anthologies by Sunbury Press, HellBound Press, Black Ink Fiction, Dragon Roost Press, *Unsettling Reads*, Phobica Books, PsychoToxin Press, Wandering Wave Press, rebellionLIT Press, *Bullet Points Vol. 3*, *Critical Blast*, Off-Topic Publishing, Exploding Head Press, Sinister Smile Press, *DraculaBeyondStoker Magazine*, *Mystery Magazine*, Headshot Press, Nightshade Press, WonderBird Press; and featured in narrative podcasts such as Zoetic Press' *Alphanumeric*, *Sudden Fictions*, and *Tales to Terrify*.

More stories released soon in the upcoming anthologies by Grendel Press, Dragon Roost Press, WriteHive, Crystal Lake Publishing, Dark Matter INK, and more.

Mia's work has been selected as *Tales to Terrify*'s top ten best stories of 2023 and shortlisted for the Crime Writers Association's Daggers Award 2024.

She is the author of the novels *Estate Sale* and *Haven*, novellas *Tell Me a Story*, *Discordant*, and *Arrokoth*, and the collection *Smile So Red and Other Tales of Madness*.

Mia has an overactive imagination, a perfect poker face, and a fondness for baked goods. When she isn't busy making things up and writing them down, she spends time with her lovely wife, reads, plays music, does crosswords, and tries to convince herself she appreciates nature.

Find her at:
Official website: https://daliaverse.wixsite.com/author
Twitter: @ Dalia_Verse
FB: DaliaVerse
Instagram: daliaverse
https://linktr.ee/daliaverse

ABOUT THE PUBLISHERS

Nate Ragolia is a lifelong lover of science fiction and its power to imagine worlds more hopeful and inclusive than the real one. His first book, *There You Feel Free*, was published by 1888's Black Hill Press in 2015. Spaceboy Books reissued it in 2021. He's also the author of *The Retroactivist* (2017). His most recent book, *One Person Can't Make a Difference* (2022), was featured on Tor.com's Can't Miss Indie Press Speculative Fiction list, and was translated into Italian for Ringworld Sci-Fi in 2023. He founded and edited *BONED*, a literary magazine, and also created two webcomics. Nate is also a husband and a dog dad.

Shaunn Grulkowski has been compared to Warren Ellis and Phillip K. Dick and was once described as what a baby conceived by Kurt Vonnegut and Margaret Atwood would turn out to be. He's at least the fifth best Slavic-Latino-American sci-fi writer in the Baltimore metro area. He's the author *Retcontinuum*, and the editor of *A Stalled Ox* and *The Goldfish* for 1888/Black Hill Press.